It's O.K., I'm A Doctor

It's O.K., I'm A Doctor

B.B. Howard

To order additional copies of this book, contact:
Xlibris Corporation
1-888-795-4274
www.Xlibris.com
Orders@Xlibris.com
51914

CONTENTS

FORWARD

I never met Paul Eldridge. I never shook his hand or got to speak to him. I know of him only through the stories told to me by one of his daughters (he has five in all). A while back, I wrote a poem for her to give to her father on his 65th birthday. The poem was just a short summary of the things that Paul treasured and enjoyed doing. It was no poetic masterpiece but Paul enjoyed it. A few months later, Paul went home to live with Jesus. At his funeral, one of Paul's son-in-laws read the little poem. For a few moments, it brought a smile to the faces of Paul's loved ones much as it had made Paul smile on his birthday. As I looked around at the tear stained eyes that were now smiling, I kept thinking to myself that I should be happy and quite proud of myself but all I could feel was shame. I had been given a small gift and had kept it to myself. I felt like the servant in the parable in the Bible who hid the talent his master had given him while the other servants invested their talents and gave them back to the master with interest. While the talent that I was given isn't literary genius, God did put within me the ability to tell a story. I would like to invest that talent in you, the reader, and hopefully return it to my master with smiles as interest. And so, this little book is a collection of the stories that have made me smile in the course of my life and are as near to the truth as I can recall. Part truth, part opinion, and part imagination, it is all written in the spirit of love. With the exception of Paul and my immediate family, the names have been changed to protect the innocent and even the not so innocent.

Note to the reader: I will meet Paul Eldridge one day.

INTRODUCTION

It's O.K., I'm a Doctor. My entire life has been a series of getting snagged on one technicality or another. My wife asked me the other day if I had taken out the trash like she had asked. I've taken out the trash hundreds of times so I say, "Sure, I've taken out the trash". She then asks if I've taken it out recently. O.K., technically I had not taken it out just then. She got me on a technicality. I really wanted to be rich and handsome but by some technical fluke, I ended up poor and homely.

So, I'm not a Doctor. I could say that I have a Ph.D. from the school of hard knocks, but that's kind of hard to prove since they don't give out diplomas, although I do have some pretty cool scars to show for it. However, none of those things translate too well onto a resume. No, I'm not a Doctor and I don't even play one on T.V., but since laughter is good medicine for the soul, if I make you laugh, then—technically—I could be considered a Doctor. Of course if you think the book is stupid, that would make me a quack.

Where do we go from here? We get through this together. Don't be afraid to laugh, I wasn't. I intended to make myself the good guy in all of these stories, but modesty (actually honesty) would not allow for it. Instead, I found that we laugh loudest when we laugh at ourselves. I have to admit that I have laughed at myself quite a bit in compiling these stories. I thought that I had been a reasonably suave kind of guy up until I remembered some of the really stupid things I did. I'll bet if you read far enough, you will run across something you have done yourself. If so, feel free to laugh and rest assured that you are not alone in the world of lunacy. I just wrote it down so the entire world could laugh with me.

I hope that when you are done, you will find humor in some of the ordinary things around you. God gave us a sense of humor, don't be afraid to use it. Trust me, I'm a Doctor

THE DIFFERENCE BETWEEN
MEN AND WOMEN

Aside from anatomy, there are some fundamental differences between the sexes. The differences do not imply superiority on either part, they merely reflect the different perspectives that each take when approaching life. Logic, for instance. The definition and rules for logic are basically the same with regards to the two genders. It is the interpretation of these rules that separates men from women. There should actually be two terms: Male logic and Female logic.

Male logic is consistent within the gender and makes sense to nearly all men. The same is true with women and female logic. The trouble arises when one group tries to understand the logic of the other. When a man sees something a woman does, he can make no sense of it because he applies his rules for logic to her decision. Never happen. The woman's decision was based on her logic. To her, her decision was clear and simple and based on pure logic. To him, her decision seems haphazard and induced by narcotics. It took me several painful years to make this discovery and so I am now passing it on to you in hopes that you may better understand your spouse.

The first time I realized that my logic did not apply to my wife was after five full years of marriage (I'm not very bright). So there I was after a hard day of working out in the yard, covered with grease and soot, proud of all that I had accomplished. I had very nearly reduced my honey-do list by one half and was exhausted. I undressed, threw my clothes in the dirty clothes hamper and took a shower. The next Saturday rolls around and, once again, I prepared to attack my ever growing honey-do list with reckless abandon. I couldn't find my favorite work pants so I asked my wife if she had seen them. She said she hadn't and asked me where I put them last. Obviously, if I knew where I put them I would know where they were. I told her I had not seen them since last Saturday when I put them in the dirty clothes hamper. A look of horror filled her face and she asked incredulously why I would put them in the dirty clothes hamper. I tell her, with no small amount of sarcasm in my voice that, in that they were both dirty and clothes, they would be more than welcome in the dirty clothes hamper. Apparently, that was not the correct answer because she then informed me that my dirty clothes were not to go into the hamper because they stink. I said of course they stink, that's how I knew they were dirty and this fact reinforced my decision to put them in the dirty clothes hamper and not to wear them again.

At this point, I was convinced that this was some cruel joke and that either the crew from Candid Camera was going to pop out or I would hear Rod Serling say, "Submitted for your approval, a man slowly losing touch with reality" as the theme from Twilight Zone becomes audible in the background and the camera pans to me laying on the floor in a puddle of drool trying to catch dust particles dancing in the light. But no, worse yet, this was real. I managed to make my eye quit twitching and wiped up most of the drool that I found running out of the corner of my mouth when my wife hit me with the big guns (they always save the big guns for last). We don't even put dirty clothes in the dirty clothes hamper. The drool floodgates opened wide and the nervous twitch in my eye turns into a complete full body tremor. With the last remaining grain of sanity, I managed to ask feebly, "why do we have a dirty clothes hamper if we don't put dirty clothes in it?". My wife looked at me in utter amazement that I could be so dense and said in that same condescending tone she uses to tell the children why they can't have another snack, "because it matches the rest of the bathroom set". I lost consciousness shortly thereafter and don't remember much of the next few days.

After several years of marriage, I thought that I pretty much figured out female logic and had it under control. It was then that I learned the error of my ways. Having observed female behavior and being a student of their logic, I knew that from time to time, they try to trip you up. Armed with this knowledge, I remained on full alert and was prepared to combat just such a situation. Then it happened, there at a craft store, my lovely bride asked me if I think the candles on sale would fit our sconces and match our color scheme. Ha—Ha—Ha. You have to get up pretty early in the morning to trick me, sister. I caught her in her little feeble attempt to trick me. I had lived in that house for years and was quite certain that we did not even have a color scheme. For crying out loud, every room in the house was a different color. How could that be a color scheme? And further more, how could she be so foolish as to use a word like "sconce"? What kind of word is "SCONCE"? That was the most stupid word I had ever heard of, surely she could come up with a more believable word than that. I decided to use my powers of gamesmanship against her. I wasn't falling for that made-up word. The tables were officially turned. I innocently asked what a sconce was just to see how quickly she could come up with some lame excuse. Without blinking an eye, she said it's one of the candle holders that hangs on the wall in the living room. She looked at me in utter disbelief that I could be so unrefined and ignorant. Her answer was quick, too quick. Maybe she had all of that thought out beforehand. She could be quite treacherous.

Just then, before I could tighten the noose around her pretty little neck, she recoils in full fury from defense to offense and said that I probably didn't even know what our color scheme was. I felt like the mouse who doesn't even know he's caught until he hears the trap spring shut just as it crushes his pointy little head. I could feel my pointy little head crushing. I said of course I know and immediately realized how embarrassing it is to be caught in a lie when your forced to guess at the answer you just swore you already knew. Trap shut, pointy little head crushed, game over.

She then went through a complete discourse on what matched in what room and how each room had its own color scheme. I was pretty sure that there couldn't be more than one color scheme per household but, apparently, that thought was flawed. On the way out of the store, I walked with my head down just a few feet behind my wife. I stayed pretty close because periodically she would think of something else I should know and then she would let me in on it. On the way out of the door, the saleswoman patted my wife on the arm and gave her that knowing look as if to say, "It is alright, hon, I've got one just like him at home". After that, we went home and I color coordinated my tools.

Truth is also a concept that varies from gender to gender. Ask a man his opinion and he will give it to you. We are basically honest like that. A woman's opinion varies depending on who is asking the question. My wife asked me if I liked her dress. I, of course, think she wants to know the truth so as not to embarrass herself in public by wearing something ugly. I answered, "No, it's ugly. It reminds me of the siding on my aunt's old house". A good, honest shot of the truth. Sometimes too much of the truth is a bad thing. That's a man's version of the truth, it is pretty much a what you see is what you get kind of thing. A woman's version is slightly different. One day my wife and I were shopping in the mall and we saw a lady friend. My wife says, "Oh, I love your hair" and they discuss the finer points of hair styling and so on and then our friend has to leave. After she left, my wife said, "Did you see that hideous monstrosity on her head? It looked like a cat got scared and ran up there and died". I replied, "I thought you said you loved her hair". "No, I was being kind", she replied. "Is it kind to let her walk around looking stupid?" I asked. "No, but I don't know her well enough to tell her that". Apparently, truth also varies with relationships as well. That concludes my argument that men are basically more honest than women.

TOP TEN THINGS NEVER TO SAY TO YOUR WIFE

1. "I never really noticed that mustache before". Self explanatory.
2. "Of course I love you, but . . ." It's over. It doesn't even matter what you follow "but" with, your wife didn't hear anything after the ill-fated "but". Just bow out gracefully, admit defeat and prepare to finance a major shopping spree.
3. "You don't look bad for a woman your age". Way to go moron. You just invoked the double jeopardy rule. You mentioned looks and age in the same breath. This statement is usually compounded by adding, "What I really meant was . . .". Don't bother. Even if you have a really great recovery line for this mess, save it. You can't get out of this hole so why waste a good excuse on a losing cause?
4. "You remind me of my mother". Your wife has spent her entire married life trying to out-do your mother and here you compare the two. Bad career move.
5. "Since you're already up . . .". To men, this seems like the perfect opportunity to ask for a snack, softdrink, toenail clippers, etc. You feel like you have been sensitive to her needs by waiting until she was already up to ask for something. The truly novice hubby will act as though this request was spontaneous and only occurred to him after he saw his wife get up. The answer is "D", none of the above. Despite what your common logic will dictate, your wife will interpret your request as you being lazy rather than sensitive to her needs. She will also conclude that you only think of her when you are hungry or thirsty and therefore, only think of her as little more than a maid. Besides that, you leave the toilet seat up.

6. Number 6 is the answer to the question, "Does this outfit make me look fat?" or any similar question. Any answer here is wrong. There is an escape route from this death trap but it requires an Academy Award winning performance, cat-like reflexes and a good deal of luck. When the deadly question is posed, you must first resist the urge to say, "No, Honey, you look fine" or the bigger urge to say, "It's not the outfit that makes you look fat, it's your big behind that makes you look fat". Speed is of the essence here, immediately conjure up a medical emergency. Leg cramps and Charlie horses are ideal for this scenario. Make a big enough scene and the question is forgotten. Even if it is not forgotten, you can always get up and pretend to walk it off, thus providing you with an excuse to leave the room.

7. "You don't sweat much for a fat woman". If you need an explanation for this one, ask the person who is helping you with the big words in this book to explain it to you.

8. "No, Honey, you go on to bed, I'm going to stay up and watch Baywatch". If you have to have your bikini fix, pretend to go to the bathroom and sneak back in the living room to the T.V. set. Keep the sound off. However, if your wife finds you watching T.V. with the sound off, there is no lie to save you.

9. "My mom never cooked it that way". This is the only stupid statement that can have positive financial results. There is no recovery from it, but if you invest in frozen food products, you will probably see sales skyrocket.

10. "I'll be home by dark". "Dark" implies a specific time. Women lock in on specifics. In your wife's mind, dark means when the sun goes down and she assigns a specific time to that. To a man, "Dark" means anytime between six p.m. and July. You feel as though you were vague enough to keep your wife from expecting you at any certain time, therefore, there is no reason for you to phone home to explain why you are late. There is a better answer that will make her happy and keep you out of trouble. "Honey, I really don't know when I'll be home and I don't want you to worry. Tell you what, I'll call every hour until I leave". Your wife will sense your sensitivity and concern for her emotional stability and say, "Oh don't be silly, just come home whenever you are done". This gives you a much larger margin of error in case the fish are biting or any other such emergency arises. This plan can backfire if you have used it too many times before. She may say, "I'd appreciate it if you call every hour" and then you are pretty much grounded for life. If this happens, hang around the house long enough to get on her nerves and you should get a reprieve.

TOP TEN THINGS NEVER TO SAY TO YOUR HUSBAND

1. "Does this outfit make me look fat?" Of course it makes you look fat. The cat still has the button embedded in its flank from the last time you tried to squeeze into those jeans. Why compound things by making your husband lie? Or worse yet, tell the truth? Besides, you dye your hair, wear fake nails, smear on makeup with a trowel, wear a push-up bra, and heels to make you look taller. Why start now asking about the truth?

2. "What time will you be home?" He's going to lie. You know he's going to lie. Why give him the chance to practice getting better at it?

3. "Do you think she is attractive?" That is not a question, it is a statement. This is another example of how men are basically more honest than women. What you are really saying is, "Lie to me now so that I can catch you and be mad. I really need something to hold over your head for the next time I want a new dress".

4. "We need to talk". This statement has the same effect as telling Superman that he has on Kryptonite underwear. To a woman this means, "We need to sit down, be serious, and discuss some weighty matter that could effect our entire life". This could include topics ranging from choosing the color of the shower curtain to naming the children. Women see this is a good thing, she and her man are going to share thoughts and ideas. They are totally confused when they see this look of impending doom on their husband's face. What women need to realize is that from their husband's first date as a teenager until he married them, "We need to talk" was always followed by, "I'd like to see other people", "I think we need to explore our options" or, "I think of you just like a brother (the ultimate kiss of death)".

5. "We never talk anymore". This is partially true. Over the years, you have continued talking but your husband has stopped listening. Men communicate in the simplest manner possible (see chapter regarding same), and discard what they feel is unnecessary information. If the truth were told, you husband hasn't heard much of what you have said since the second week you were married. He gets most of the big stuff, usually.

6. "Are you really going to wear that?" Keep in mind that men have a very delicate ego and he really thinks those bell bottoms still look good. You and I both know that polyester is out, just don't tell him.

7. "What is more important, me or that game on T.V.?" Don't put him in a position to make decisions while he is distracted. It is just not fair.

8. "Which outfit would look better?" you have spent the entirety of your married life telling your husband that he should be arrested for fashion felony and you will further reinforce this notion in his mind by wearing the exact opposite of his selection for you.

9. "Did you leave the toilet seat up?" No, the same person who lost the T.V. remote control and took the odd sock out of the laundry left the toilet seat up. Of course he left it up. You know he left it up and now here is the Earth shattering news that all wives need to know: Your husband left the toilet seat up because he went to sleep in his recliner watching Letterman. He woke up, went to the restroom, and simply forgot to put the seat down. He did not leave it up because he is an insensitive jerk who doesn't care about you and is not now giggling to himself at the thought of you taking the Tidybowl plunge. There is no conspiracy, no malice aforethought, no intent. Nothing. Nada. Zip. Period. End of story. Please spread the word.

10. "You are right". Never, I repeat, never say this to your husband. He simply can not stand the shock to his system. Keep blaming him for everything, he already knows how those rules work.

WHY MEN HATE CARDS

Ladies, pay attention, men hate cards. It's nothing personal, we just hate them. My wife thinks that nothing says, "I love you" like a nice card. Listen, nothing says, "I love you" like saying, "I love you" and it doesn't cost a dime. Men are basically dumb and honest creatures. We are not terribly sophisticated and often have a difficult time grasping the symbolism and subtle suggestions that most cards wreak of. We really only want the honest truth from the one we love, not from some guy who goes to work every day and tries to think of new and creative ways to say, "I love you" so that Hallmark can charge you $4.95. Besides, that same guy has two martinis for lunch and then goes home, kicks his dog and sits around in his underwear watching ESPN like the rest of us slobs.

The very first time Uncle Sam sent me overseas, we were gone for 30 days before we got our first mail. I was young, newlywed and really missing my wife when the mail finally came. My letter was huge. It was three times as thick as everyone else's and I was the object of much envy among my fellow mail recipients. My mind raced at the endless possibilities, there could be pictures inside wrapped by a monstrous five page letter, there could be newspaper clippings telling me of Earth shattering events that I had missed while at sea, short of baked goods, there could be almost anything inside.

I hurried to my little rack, climbed inside, shut the curtains, turned on my light and prepared myself so that I might savor each and every delight that awaited me. I had to take a deep breath to calm myself. I felt as though I might pass out. I wasn't sure if this was from the sheer excitement of hearing from home or from the guy's socks hanging from the bunk above me. At any rate, I was exhilarated and more excited than at any other event I could recall. I started what would later become a ritual over the next few years of my travels. I first looked at the postmark. I would calculate how long it had taken to get to me and try to remember where I was when my wife sent it. For some reason, the postmark thing became an obsession. We would all sit around and see whose letter had taken the longest to get there. The next phase was to look at my wife's handwriting on the envelope. It was so delicate and precise. It only seemed natural that a girl so lovely would write so gracefully. The last step prior to reading my letter, which I repeated after I had read my letter, was to smell the perfume my wife had sprayed on it. I could close my eyes and for the most fleeting second, my wife would be in my arms and there was no ship, no foreign country, nothing but me and my girl. But then I would open my eyes and only her fragrance would linger and no matter how many times I tried to close my eyes and recapture her, she was gone. All that remained was her card, words from her heart to mine. The most intimate conversation two people in love can share across an ocean.

With all the restraint of a child on Christmas morning, I opened my letter from home. What had once been filled with endless possibilities, became a lousy card. A huge, lousy card. It had pages and pages. I flipped through each page hoping to find a folded note, a picture, anything. I finally came to the last page and saw the familiar, lovely handwriting. At last, no need to panic. There is word from home after all. I calmed myself, brought the card close and read the words, "Love, Amber". Love, Amber! Love, Amber? What is that? I'd been gone a month, the only thread of sanity was the hope that I'd hear from my beautiful bride. I longed for words of encouragement, hope, news from the States, anything. Instead, I got, "Love, Amber".

My wife and I have had many conversations in the years since then about cards but I still don't think she gets the picture. Recently, she gave a friend a birthday present. A few days later she received a "Thank You" card. She said, "This is the sweetest card I've ever gotten, I'm going to call her and thank her". I sarcastically said, "Maybe you should just send a card". She did. Most men aren't smart enough to remember whose turn it is to send a card and who did what nice thing. Besides, men are much more effective communicators and say all that needs to be said right then, no card written by some nerdy computer geek at Hallmark. Man's answer to the card problem is as follows: "Hey Hank, I saw you were leaking some transmission fluid. Let's drop that bad boy and see if we can fix it". Hank's response (this may seem a tad bit mushy but men can be sensitive too): "Thanks, Bob, I owe you one buddy". An overly affectionate man might even add a gentle punch to the shoulder but never, under any circumstances, would he send a card. No cards!

COMMUNICATION:
MEN VS WOMEN

Now for the unbridled truth that will seem blasphemous to all women; stay with me, I can prove my point. Men are better communicators than women. Yes, I know what I just said, I'm the one who said it. Men really are better at communication than women. One of the basic constructs of intelligence is the ability to communicate. The more efficient the communication, the more intelligence is required. I will only comment on the communication aspect here, you can draw your own conclusions about the intelligence part.

Men communicate in the simplest of terms in a one-dimensional manner. In other words, when a man gives an answer, that is the answer. There is no hidden agenda behind his words, there is no double meaning or symbolic suggestions, what he says is what he means. Women, on the other hand, communicate on multi-dimensional levels. What they say has nothing to do with what they mean. This is where their communication system is flawed. This leaves them open for misinterpretation at every level and thus, error at every level. Without digressing any further into the psychobabble depths, I will diagram a conversation between a man and his wife to demonstrate my point. I realize that this may be more science than you thought you were getting into but it never hurts to learn. For the purpose of this lesson, M = Male and F = Female.

F: Honey, do you want to go to my parent's house for Thanksgiving?
M: Sure.
F: You know that you don't.
M: If you know that I don't, then why would you ask?
F: To see what you would say.
M: Well, I said, "Yes".

F: But you really don't.
M: OK, I don't.
F: See, I told you that you really didn't want to go.
M: Look, I want to go, why would I lie to you?
F: To keep me from being mad.
M: Honey, I always tell you the truth, you can ask me anything.
F: OK, did you like supper tonight?
M: No.
F: Why not? You love my ham.
M: It was too salty.
F: You like it salty.
M: I like it salted, not salty.
F: Great, what else have you been keeping from me?
M: I haven't been keeping anything from you. Just forget it, can we get back to Thanksgiving?
F: I'm not going anywhere with someone who lies to me and hates my cooking.
M: Fine.
F: Sure, you get your way. You always get your way. We never get to do anything I want to do. All I wanted to do was to go see my folks for the Holidays. Just forget It, sniff, sniff.
M: C'mon Honey. You know that I want to do whatever will make you happy. You know that I think you are the most beautiful woman in the world. We can do whatever you want for thanksgiving.
F: Really, you think that I am beautiful?
M: Yes, you are the most beautiful woman in the world.
F: Am I prettier than Jennifer Aniston?
M: Of course.
F: Liar.
M: OK, but you're a close second.
F: Sniff, sniff, then get Jennifer Aniston to make your salted ham.

Another example is the time I asked my wife what she wanted for Mother's Day. "Oh, nothing", she said, "Save your money". Me, being an idiot, got her nothing. Mother's Day rolled around and she asked me what I got her. "Nothing", I tell her and reminded her that she said she didn't want anything. "And you believed me?" she cried. This is a perfect illustration of the multi-dimensional levels on which women communicate. First, there is the literal level. In this example, "Nothing" was the literal answer to what my wife said she wanted for Mother's Day. Second was the implied level. While she said she wanted nothing, she actually implied that she wanted a gift. Finally, is the preferred level which is where she is actually saying, "Of course I want something, and if you were really in tune with me, you wouldn't even have to ask". One woman, three levels.

Ask me what I want. The list is endless. That is because men are better communicators than women. Ask a question, we give you an answer. By the way, I'd like a bass boat, a new truck, a box of shotgun shells or anything made of camouflage.

Back to science. Once, as a young man, I had the opportunity to work off-shore on a rig in the Gulf of Mexico. Two men lived in a tiny building on that rig for a month at a time and then came home for a month. I watched then while we worked on the rig. The never spoke to one another, yet they knew what the other wanted and when. Over supper, one handed the catsup to the other without ever even looking at him or even uttering a word. Women would say that this shows a lack of communication skills and is barbaric. I say that this was communication at its highest and most efficient level. They moved past the spoken word to communicate. Quite frankly, this would kill most women that I know.

Communication is most efficient when it is simple. Less room for interpretation. Ironically, this is the very reason that most women criticize men for their lack of communication skills. It is not that we don't communicate well, we simply do it more efficiently than they do. Most of the time a simple, "Yes" or "No" will do. Everything after that just clouds the facts with irrelevant details. Take for instance a football game. After a game winning touchdown run, a man will say something to the effect of, "Nice run". He definitely won't say, "What a beautiful run, he really overcame the obstacles of his childhood to accomplish this great feat. He really deserves to succeed". Truth is, "Nice run" sums it up nicely. Everything after that is just window dressing.

Women, I hope that I have convinced you that men really can communicate with you. Remember, what he says is what he means. Anything else that you read into it was conjured up in you mind not his. If you ever grasp this simple point, please share it with my wife.

DRIVING MISS AMBER

Lest you think that I am complaining, let me start by saying that my wife is very nearly perfect. She is everything that a man could possibly want in a wife. She is attractive, a great cook, pretty good fisherman, loves sports and likes carnations better than roses. She is thoughtful and understands when I am not. She puts up with me, and that, in itself, is a minor miracle. She sends cards and signs my name. When I made my last cruise, she sent self-addressed, stamped envelopes complete with the appropriate holiday card inside. All I had to do was sign them and drop them in the mail. Just for the record, I managed to get all of those out on time. She is by far my better half, in fact, she's about my better three quarters. So what could I possibly have to complain about? Read on.

In our house, at any given time, there are no less than three full cases of soda. She has her favorite, I have my favorite and there is at least one case for the kids. Despite the fact that we live in a rural area, we also have the technology available to make ice. Having said this, most people would generally agree that we have all the makings of a decent cold drink (I didn't mention that we also have cups, I thought that was a given). So, what are the first words out of her mouth when we get in the car for a road trip? "I want a coke", I point out that we have roughly 27 gallons of soft drink available just inside our house. "I want one with ice" is her usual reply. Again, I point out that we have ice in our humble abode. "I want crushed ice", is the next part of the conversation. I remind her that I have no less than five hammers, but to no avail. We drive the required three blocks to the nearest convenient store with the highest mark-up on drinks in seventeen counties. Twelve dollars later, we are now ready to begin our trip. Fear not the idea of going hungry, we have a ready supply of potato chips, snacks, candy bars and jerky.

Off we go into the wild blue yonder of travel. Out on the open road, nothing but the wail of the radio and the whine of the tires to keep us company. Out with the big rigs, out to the first roadside stop we can find. This usually takes about eight minutes from the time we leave our driveway but never happens until we have just left the city limits of the last town for one hundred miles. Then, those words that every man hates to hear, "I need to stop and use the restroom". "Where do you want to stop" I always patiently ask. "Somewhere that I can get a Coke" is the usual answer.

I gave up fighting about a year after I got married. I soon realized that a long trip with a miserable woman is a long, miserable trip. Then I decided to drive at night. That way everyone could sleep. This, I reasoned, would make a much more pleasant trip. Our first late night excursion arrived, we load up with convenience store junk food, and off we go. I suggested to my wife that she try to get some sleep. "You know that I can't sleep in the car", she said. "Well try", I tell her as we cruise along. About two minutes later, the sound of the radio is drowned out by the roar of her snoring and the thud of her head hitting the window as it bobs in rhythm to the whining tires.

I tried to find an old country radio station that I could sing with to keep me awake. "Could you turn that down?", she mumbles in a crank voice. "I was almost asleep". You truly have to love someone to make a road trip with them. The sight of drool on your window and the sound of snoring for hours on end is enough to grate on anyone's nerves. So down goes the volume of the radio with my singing in tow. A couple of hours later, when I'm good and tired, she woke up. "I gotta go to the restroom", she announces. I asked her where she wanted to pull over. "Somewhere that I can get a Coke", she answered. We stopped, she takes care of her pressing needs and I clean candy wrappers out of the car. I asked her how she felt, "Not too good", she answers. "You know that I can't sleep in the car". Oh yeah, I forgot.

About midway through our trip, we have the same fight that we have on every trip over thirty minutes long. "Why are you mad at me?" she will ask. "I'm not mad, I just get tired of spending more of drinks and snacks than we do on gas and then stopping every eight telephone poles to go to the restroom". "Fine", she'll say, "I won't ask to stop again until we get there, will that make you happy?" I said yes but my heart wasn't really in it. That's because it was just about that time that I realized that we were only half way through the trip and I really had to go to the restroom.

THE GAME

In my younger, more athletic days of college, I used to go to a small park with my college roommates to live out our basketball fantasies. We dreamed of soaring like Jordan as we slammed over the younger competition from the local high school. If only for a few moments, we got to be like Mike. These trips became a frequent source of after-school entertainment that we labeled "Ego Ball". After a couple of hours of high flying and high fiving, we could go back to our dorm room and rest assured that we had lost none of our athletic prowess despite those few extra mid-section pounds courtesy of the local pizza place. The male ego is especially vulnerable during early adulthood and these trips had a remarkably therapeutic effect on our collective opinions of ourselves. For this reason, we ignored the fact that most of the high school kids were too short or clumsy to play at the bigger playground next to the school and, did I mention that we were playing on an eight foot goal? Probably not.

At any rate, it was about this time that I made the acquaintance of a young lady who was obviously impressed with my athletic physique, boyish charm and rugged good looks. She asked to go along on one of our "ego ball" excursions to watch. While this was normally a male only outing, I decided to let her tag along and witness, first hand, my unsurpassed skills and my cute legs in my oh-so-stylish corduroy shorts. She was naturally impressed and asked if I could take her sometime and give her some pointers. Obviously, the corduroy shorts had the desired results and the first sunny day found us on the playground—alone.

She tried a few shots and pouted when she couldn't get the ball up to the rim and I quickly realized that this had the potential for me to spend numerous hours with her, in close physical proximity, teaching her something that I did pretty well. For a while, she struggled and I showed her how to stand, where to put her feet, how to follow through and everything else she needed to know. It absolutely amazed me that even when she missed, she looked great doing it. Life was great. I looked incredibly sensitive (women love that stuff) and nurturing, and I was playing ball and spending time with a gorgeous girl. As I reflected on my good fortune, she asked if I'd like to play a game. I knew that this had the smell of danger about it. If I won, I would hurt her feelings. If she won, she would know that I let her win and would think that I was patronizing her and then she'd be mad. I tried to beg off but she insisted. She even wanted to bet an ice cream on it. I knew trouble was lurking in the shadows but was confident that my boyish charm would smooth over any hurt feelings, besides, I love ice cream. Always the gentleman, I offered to let her have the ball first. As she declined, she dribbled the ball behind her back and then between her legs and said she would shoot for it. While somewhat taken aback, I was nonetheless undaunted and quite confident that I could handle a girl on the playground. Besides, she was way too cute to be very good. She hit the first five in a row from the three-point line (college, not pro) so I decided that it was in my best interest to play up close and put a little pressure on her. Use the old intimidation factor, scare her a little. So, I closed the clamps, using a smother defense, I clamped down on her like a vise. I didn't want to flex my basketball muscle but it was time to make a statement. I saw the fear in her eyes as she tensed with panic. At first, I thought I had gone too far. Then, after the headfake, crossover dribble and ensuing layup, I realized that I had been had. At this point, I think that I should point out that, until that moment, I had always viewed the fairer sex as beautiful creatures to be treasured and not treated as competitors. I mean, after all, I was raised in the deep South. We still say "Ma'am" and open doors for ladies. My upbringing was firmly rooted in the rich, Southern heritage of chivalry. And so, with all the gallantry that I could muster, I did what any true Southern gentleman would do, I fouled her. I fouled her hard. Real hard. Too late I realized that being cute did not hinder her from being tough as well. Her next drive to the basket was complete with not only a mean crossover dribble, but a well placed forearm to my chest.

Fortunately for her, just as I was about to unleash an arsenal of jumpshots and layups, I pulled a hamstring and had to call the game. I could see she was disappointed but to come back and defeat her would have crushed her and could have possibly had a negative impact on our budding relationship. Ever the consummate gentleman, I still bought the ice cream though we never actually completed the game (that means that, technically, I didn't lose).

As a boy, my dad told me that the reason Tom Landry . . . pause . . . sniff, sniff . . . O.K., Texans may now remove their hats from over their hearts, wipe the tears away, sit down and continue reading . . . was so successful was because he surrounded himself with winners. I remembered that story and decided to team up with the cute little red head with the great jumpshot (and above average forearm) and so, for the better part of my adult life, she has been my wife, partner and best friend. I always wondered why she stayed with me. Her only response was that she heard the Coach Landry story too late. Three children later, she's still gorgeous with a great jumper but my hamstring still acts up when we play.

MAMAW

I grew up on the gulf coast of Texas. The only natural resources to speak of were mosquitoes and hurricanes. With nothing else to brag on, we named a festival after the little blood sucking varmits and just plain ran from the hurricanes. During one of our hurricane episodes, with the flood waters rising and beginning to enter the house. My grandmother stopped and said, "Thank you, Lord". My great-grandmother was still living then and she asked, "Child, have you lost your mind? Your house is flooding and everything that you own is about to be destroyed". "Mother", she replied, "God tells us to give thanks in all things, even the bad times". I was just a little fellow then but it was a lesson that stuck with me. A couple of years ago, God decided that her work on Earth was done and He took her home to be with Him. When my dad called to tell me she was gone, all I could say was "Thank you".

Traveling around the world and living in different geographic regions of the country afforded me the opportunity to meet many different types of people with all types of backgrounds. I would like to think that I learned something from each of them and that each one helped to make me a better man. Too often, the lessons I have learned only prove to me how much I don't already know. This was never more clearly demonstrated to me than one morning while walking to my first college class of the day. It was spring and the day before had been in the eighties, warm for that time of the year in Arkansas. The night before I bathed and dressed for bed, it occurred to me early in my college career that I could actually sleep in the same clothes I was going to wear to school the next morning. Not only would this allow me to save time in the morning (translation = sleep late), it also let me enjoy the slob look which was the predecessor to the grunge look. I got up early the next morning and walked the short mile to school. I was wearing shorts and a T-shirt and it was getting cool. I didn't mind the cool air because I knew that by the time my first class was over, the weather would be warm and the fish would be biting at the lake. About half way to school, it started to rain and it didn't take long before I started some heavy duty pouting. You can imagine my surprise when the rain turned to snow. My pouting went into overdrive and twice I tripped on my own lip which was resting firmly on the ground. I soon began cursing the day when I left my beloved Texas for the foreign land of Arkansas. It never got that cold on the gulf coast and in Texas, when it gets hot, it stays hot.

As I approached the hill where my class was, I noticed the fresh blanket of snow on the dark green grass. About that time, I saw a young man in a wheelchair. His withered body looked pitiful sitting in that chair and he was struggling mightily to get up the hill. I saw this as my chance to do something for someone less fortunate than myself. My mood began to brighten. I was about to do my good deed for the day. I asked him if I could help him up the hill. He said he would appreciate the help. In a fairly feeble attempt at small-talk, I commented how tough it must be trying to get up the hill in that chair and how rotten the timing was for it to rain. He said he didn't mind the hill because the snow made it look awfully pretty and we really did need the rain. Great, a guy in a wheelchair going uphill in the snow could find beauty in the weather and all I could do was pout. My chance to be a do-gooder turned into my chance to prove what a self-centered jerk I really am.

In the years since, I have often thought how rotten life was treating me and that I really deserved better. Then, a memory from deep in the mountains of Arkansas slowly pushes itself to the front of my consciousness and reminds me of a hill covered in snow and a young man in a wheelchair. I really wish that I had told him "Thank You".

CHANGES

In regards to change, I am most definitely a 90's man. It's either the 1790's or 1890's depending on how progressive I feel at the moment. Some see change as a threat to the stability of their world, others embrace changes as a chance to display their coping skills and relish the opportunity to enjoy new life experiences. I subscribe to neither theory. Change requires energy and an open mind. I possess neither. My attitude towards change may not have been so skewed had it not been for a traumatic event that took place during my impressionable teenage years. My trust was completely shattered. The optimism of youth was replaced with an intense pessimism that has permeated my very being since that time. There seemed to be no belief, institution or truth that was, in itself, absolute and beyond change. This life shattering event was the precursor to many, more subtle, though no less destructive, changes. The first was so destructive that it threatened to undermine the very roots of American culture. Of course the people at Coca Cola eventually went back to the original formula but, by then, the damage was done leaving an entire generation of us with nowhere to turn for stability. It was pretty much down hill after that. Now, Snoopy advertises life insurance and Bugs and Daffy have a bank card commercial. Is nothing sacred? What's next? Will June Cleaver pose for Playboy? Will the Lone Ranger advertise for a laxative? The icons from my childhood have been exposed for the money grubbing, sellout, over-commercialized phonies that they truly are. All that is left behind is a pile of sales receipts and my shattered childhood.

I have always been led to believe that change was to simplify things and make them easier. This has not proven true where I have observed change in my life. We now supposedly live in the information age. Unfortunately for those of us clinging desperately to the past, you have to have a PHD in computer science to access all of this information. At this point, it seems only fitting that I should mention that I am computer illiterate. I thought that a web crawler was what a mechanic used to get under Spiderman's care. Had it not been for patient guidance from my nine-year old son, my VCR would still be blinking 12:00.

Computers have even invaded the workplace. At a recent job interview, the guy asked me if I could use a computer. Remembering the VCR incident, I told him that I had some programming experience. He asked me what languages I used. I told him that I had English down pat and that I didn't like to brag but I could order lunch and ask for the restroom in most Mexican restaurants. That concluded our interview.

I guess there are some advantages to all of this new technology. For instance, when my 11 year old paper boy kept throwing the paper in the flowers, one voice mail to his cell phone straightened things right out. My new cordless phone not only works well as a phone, but I can turn on the television and change channels with it as well. With a mini refrigerator and a portable potty, I could stay on the couch indefinitely.

Another change which has shaken me down to my not-so-sturdy foundation is the complete upheaval of male and female roles. As a child growing up in the South, things were pretty clearly defined. Guys did guy things and girls did girl things. When and why did guys start wearing earrings? Was there a memo and I missed it? Sure, Nameth wore panty hose on T.V., but it was only a commercial and, to the best of my knowledge, he has since refrained from any more such deviant behavior.

If, at this point, you are a feminine activist, please hear me out before you scurry off in a rampage to your nearest sexist male swine book burning location. I am all for equal rights and equal pay and am firmly against sexual harassment. Heck, both my mother and my wife are women. I am merely confused by some shifting trends and honestly believe that there are some areas that should be occupied by men and some that should be occupied by women. This is not because women are incapable but, simply stated, the physical differences (which I, for one, greatly appreciate) make them impractical to be performed by women. Let's take sports broadcasting, for instance. Men watch sports in order to enjoy the sport for the sake of the sport itself. A beautiful woman announcing a sporting event does not enhance the event. Rather, the attention is drawn to the announcer. It's not her fault, God made the female of the species more attractive so that the male of the species would notice her. Maybe we weren't bright enough to notice otherwise. No man will ever watch a football game and say, "Man, that John Madden looks good! He does that sweater great justice".

Barber shops are another area that only men should occupy. I remember as a child sitting in the barber shop with my father. Every walk of life was represented. There were businessmen, farmers, ranchers, construction workers and insurance salesmen. It was a veritable job fare for a young man. There was always a guy sitting there when you walked in who would still be there when you left. He was the resident expert on the weather, where the fish were biting, the Cowboys and the stockmarket. When the chair was empty, he would always say, "go ahead". To the best of my knowledge, he never left the place or even got a haircut for that matter but he was always there conducting the business of male bonding and generally making you feel lucky to be a guy. Now guys go to unisex salons and have women styling their hair. Worse yet is the hairdresser named Ramon who views your hair as a challenge but still envisions a work of art in the making. As for me, I want a barber, not a hairdresser. I want him to have a sturdy sounding name like Buck or Gus. No frills, just take a little off the ears.

While I'm rambling, who changed the English language when I wasn't looking? Once upon a time, something you bought and then sold later was considered "used". Now, this same item is "previously owned". Where did all of the new and improved stuff come from? What were we using before, old and junky? Remember when a prefabricated, movable dwelling was called a trailer and parked in a trailer park frequented by tornadoes? The change in language gave rise to a horrific attack on American morals and sensibilities. This attack being labeled, "Political Correctness". Probably the greatest contradiction in terms, politically correct is about as accurate as bureaucratic efficiency and military intelligence. The substance of a subject has not changed, merely the name. There are no more men and women, there are persons. The entire descriptive world has been reduced to a mass of gray ambiguity. Sharp differences are shaved away to create a world where nothing stands out and all blends together into a glob of mediocrity. I, for one, appreciate differences. I enjoy the fact that my wife does not look or smell like me. To me, she is not a person, she is a woman, and a beautiful one at that. She is a wife, not a significant other or cohabitator. None of these facts are politically correct, but they are facts none the less. Political correctness does not pretend to change the facts, merely our perspective of them. Of course, the up side to this is that is sounds much better for me to be a vertically restricted, dietetically challenged, person of other than African, Asian, or Hispanic origin than a short, fat, white guy.

Just for the record, I am not politically correct. I don't believe in welfare, quotas, affirmative action or anything that treats a human being as a color rather than a human. I am a heterosexual man in a monogamous relationship with a woman who, not coincidentally, is my wife. I like to hunt and fish and have, on occasion, killed Bambi. I would have got Thumper too if I had the chance. If I watch the news on television, I am led to believe that I am in a distinct minority in this country. Of course the same media would have me to believe that all black males are drug dealers and that all professional women are lesbians and all white people belong to hate groups. I don't believe that everyone in the South is prejudice (I had a Yankee in my house once), or that all minorities are on welfare. I think that most people, of all colors, get up in the morning, kiss their families goodbye and then go to work. Those same people do not sell drugs, have affairs, blow up Post Offices, kidnap people or belong to the Klan. Yes, I think there are a lot of ordinary people, just like me. We just don't make the news. I guess it would be pretty boring without stories of alien invasions and two-headed, lesbian serial killers. Still, it would be nice to hear about Mr. Jackson dropping off his daughter at daycare on the way to work, or about Mrs. Garcia helping with her son's soccer team.

SISTER BEULAH

In the small town where I grew up, we were one hour behind New York time and about twenty years behind in social terms. County fairs, school carnivals and hay rides were big time entertainment and most of our social activities revolved around our little country church. Most of my friends went to church with me and most of the mischief I found myself in involved them as well. It was usually their fault that I wound up in trouble, at least that is what I told my parents. We went to school together, played together and even went of vacation together. It was kind of like Ozzie and Harriet moved out west.

While there are many advantages to growing up in a small town, there are a few drawbacks. For one, you could never do anything, good or bad, without everybody and their grandmother knowing about it. Another drawback that I discovered was that all of my friends from church and I had parents who were children of the 60's. While we didn't all live in a commune and share garden space, our parents did take a community property approach to child raising. This, simply stated, meant that any parent close enough to a misbehaving child could whip them. My parents, their parents, any parents, they all whipped us. Today, the politically correct term for whipping, which is a politically incorrect action, is corporal punishment. Then, it was whipping. We didn't even get a "spanking", that was for rich kids who had nannies, we got whipped. As far as I can tell, it didn't scar me psychologically or give me a deep seated hatred for my parents, but I did learn not to misbehave. It was bad enough to have your own parents whip you, but it was doubly bad to have someone else's parents whip you. Then, you got another one at home for acting up in front of someone else. Apparently, the double jeopardy rule doesn't apply to kids.

Another, more sinister form of punishment, came in the form of one Sister Buelah Ridenbach. She was the master of the fatal glare. It was the

look that seared its way across the sanctuary to whichever child happened
to be misbehaving at the time. The glare killed all those that got in its path
and left many a disfigured child writhing in pain. All those in its path knew
to move quickly or risk permanent damage. Once, sister Agnew wasn't
paying attention and the glare burned a hole right through her blue-tinted
hair. It wasn't pretty. Given her destructive powers, you would think that
Sister Beulah would look like a monstrous creature complete with tentacles
and fangs. Instead, she was a quite pleasant looking woman with no visible
claws or anything. Monday through Saturday she was a mild mannered
mother (try saying that three times fast) who turned into the Enforcer come
Sunday morning. She was like a combination of Debbie Boone and Charles
Bronson in a South East Texas version of "Death Wish in the Sanctuary,
the Trilogy".

Sister Beulah enhanced her glare with a single raised eyebrow. Rumor
was that she used to raise both eyebrows but the destruction was so
devastating that Congress outlawed it to avoid escalating the Cold War.
It was just a rumor, but none of us doubted it. Truth be told, we were all
afraid of Sister Beulah. Even the older kids, that I knew for a fact were
tough, were afraid of her. She was not just a one-dimensional torture expert,
she had other ways of making you behave. Once we got smart enough to
avoid the glare, she would get up and come sit beside the offending child.
Then, she would pinch you. For a little woman, she had a death grip.
This did nothing but enhance her image as the Enforcer. If she ever came
and sat by you in church, you were sure to get a whipping when you got
home. Even if you showed your parents the bruise on your arm, you still
got a whipping.

We all thought that no one, except the preacher, was immune from her
glare. We had even seen the preacher flinch when he saw the glare go across
the room but we figured he was safe from harm. So did he. Then one fateful
Sunday morning, Sister Beulah stayed in the choir loft during preaching to
have a bird's eye view of us. I don't remember the exact sequence of events
after that, but I do know that Quinton dropped a hymnal, Shelly giggled,
Sister Beulah glared and the preacher didn't move. He really should have
moved. We couldn't get anyone to preach his funeral, I guess word had
gotten out. Instead of a funeral, we just had a time of testimony and a pot
luck lunch (after all, it was a Baptist church).

When I got a little older, I decided that it was time to assert my manhood.
I was, after all, pretty much grown. I had a few hairs on my chin and three
on my chest. I was ready for a showdown. Never one to underestimate my

opponent, I decided that the best way to fight fire was with fire. I sat in front of the mirror and practiced the glare for hours. No matter how I contorted my face, I couldn't get that eyebrow to budge. Nope, that sucker wasn't moving. I scrunched and squinted but could not make that eyebrow arch even the slightest inch. It did move once but my brother said that I didn't look scary, he said that I looked like I had gas. Not exactly the look I was going for. After forty-five minutes, I gave up with a headache. Undaunted, I decided to press forward without the eyebrow thing.

The next Sunday I got my chance. Shelly giggled, she always giggled, and Sister Beulah looked our way. I braced myself and prepared to meet her glare. My muscles tensed, my upper lip stiffened and my backbone was straight. My eyes met hers, my muscles sagged, my upper lip dropped and backbone, courage and knees all buckled simultaneously. Yes, in the moment of truth, I flinched. My friends all tried to console me though they did so very quietly. No sense in all of us being humiliated in one Sunday. It took me several years, but I finally got over that experience. OK, I was in counseling for quite a while, but that was a very traumatic experience. Just about the time I quit having bad dreams, I met my wife. She can do the eyebrow thing too. Sometimes you just can't win.

One Sunday evening, we were sitting in church and trying our best to behave. Sister Beulah's husband, Gerald, was sitting in his usual pew playing with rubber bands that he had wrapped around his hand. Every parent in the room looked back at their child when the three rubber bands went flying and nailed the preacher squarely in the center of his forehead. We were all desperately proclaiming our innocence to our parents with our pleading eyes as they mouthed various threats about what was going to happen to us when we got home. I'm not sure how anyone figured out who fired the shots, all we knew was that we were truly innocent (this time). We knew that the behind whipping possibilities far outweighed the humor so we stayed quiet. Besides, we were as curious as our parents as to the identity of the rubber band bandit. The preacher got up and looked straight at Gerald. There was a look of genuine pity on his face as he acknowledged his assailant. He said that he had been ignored, walked out on and contradicted; just never shot at. As far as he was concerned, he had reached another milestone in his preaching career. Everyone in the congregation laughed except for Sister Beulah. Her face turned an indignant shade of crimson and poor Gerald just grimaced. We all wondered if it was from embarrassment or if Sister Beulah had used the pinching treatment on him during the prayer. I don't know which it was but Gerald never had rubber bands in church again and the young preacher soon gave up the ministry and now runs a cleaning service somewhere in North Texas.

Sister Beulah wasn't the only one who dealt out punishment. Like I sad, we were a community property church in that respect. One sad day in my life, I had the misfortune of taking Quinton's advice. We had a work day at the church which were usually pretty cool because we ate a big meal after working. One this particular day, Quinton and I decided to paint the eve up on the Education Wing. The "Education Wing" is what we called the classrooms where Sunday School was held after we remodeled. Before we remodeled, it was just called the "Classrooms". The Education Wing had a small roof that extended out from the main roof over the sidewalk in front of the classrooms, excuse me, the Education Wing. Both roofs had an eve but to do the one on top, we had to get on top of the roof. That job was for me and Quinton. You could see for miles from up there. You could spit down or throw things at people and they would never know who did it. After the spitting and throwing and looking, we got to some serious painting. About half way through the project, Quinton pointed out that it would probably be years until we repainted that eve. His logic continued that since no one could see us throwing stuff at them from up there, they couldn't see what we painted either. So far, I was following him and he was making pretty good sense. Further, he continued, we ought to let the next folks that painted the eve know who did it last (meaning us). Now he was making good sense. So we decided to paint our names on the eve, not as an act of vandalism, but just to mark our place in church history. It was really out of reverence to the work that we did it. Nothing malicious or disrespectful intended. We did a wonderful paint job and then signed it. All in all, pretty tasteful. Nothing gaudy or showy, just our names and the date saved for posterity. We got down on the ground and looked up at it from all angles. Sure enough, you couldn't see it from the ground. Old Quinton was pretty good at figuring out stuff like that. Sure enough, I had to take my hat off to Quinton, you couldn't see a thing from the ground at all. Now from the road, that was a different story entirely. My dad, Quinton's dad and every other dad saw our handiwork from the road driving in to church. Both our dads whipped us. Quinton wasn't looking so smart after all. Then, after everyone had seen our little contribution to art and posterity, the entire church got together to decide what needed to be done. Being Baptist, they formed a committee. It was called the Discipline Review Committee, I think they still have it today. Still being Baptist, they had a pot luck dinner while they decided our fate. Fist, Brother Ed said that maybe we should be tarred and feathered. Then the preacher, Brother Leroy, says that is out of the question. Good for him, says I. Besides, Brother Leroy points out, that would ruin the new upholstery on the pews. Next, Sister Iona says that they ought to line us up and let the entire church whip us and I really didn't think a repeat performance of my earlier whipping could make me repent any more than I already had. Quinton looks over at me and his expression tells me that we are pretty much done for. Quinton kind of has a way about knowing when you were in big trouble. Just about the time the committee starts to look like a lynch mob, a voice from the back of the room says, "No, I think these boys have suffered enough. Boys, let this be a lesson to you not to misbehave anymore. Go on now and straighten up". The rest of the adults reluctantly nodded and then slowly disbanded leaving us with our guilty consciences and the woman whose words had saved us, good old Sister Beulah.

A little while back, I went to a church reunion back in my hometown. Memories came flooding back as I sat in the same old pews where I got into so much trouble and had so much fun. One of life's greatest fears came to life when I realized that I was in a room full of people who could tell my children stories of my misbehavior. Yes, it had the potential to get ugly. Yet, as I looked around the room, all I could see were old familiar faces full of love. They even had the pictures of old church members that had gone Home to be with the Lord a couple of which had fallen victim to the glare. I looked across the room and saw Sister Beulah. She looked so sweet and kind, I couldn't believe that I had ever been afraid of her. She looked like the president of the P.T.A. sitting over there so innocently. I started to get up and go say hello to her but, just as I got up, her eyes met mine and once again I was nine years old and my knees buckled. Big deal, I flinched. Anyway, it was a nice thought.

I now have three children truly created in their father's image. From time to time, I have to get on to them in church. In case I never get the chance, this side of Heaven, let me say "Thank You" Sister Beulah for helping to make me a decent kid and a pretty good dad along the way.

DOGS, CATS & ALL OTHERS

I have spent the biggest portion of my life studying human nature, both formally and informally. I have a degree that says that I know all about humans and their behavior and am working on others to further confirm my expertise in human nature. The biggest problem that I have encountered is that my life experience is at odds with my formal training. Conventional wisdom, as it is written in all of my over-priced textbooks, tells me that people are, in fact, individuals and can not be lumped together into groups. I can not believe this in light of all of my life experiences to the contrary. I firmly believe that upon completion of my final degree, that I will walk across the podium and shake hands with Dr. Degree-giver who will lean over and say, "We were all kidding about that stereotype thing, but don't tell anyone". All will then make sense and be right with the world. Until such time as that happens, I will continue to spread the word to anyone who will listen. And so, dear reader, for the first time in your entire life, you will see the truth laid out before you like vast riches there for you alone to seize. The truth is as follows: there are only three kinds of people in this world; dog people, cat people, and an eclectic group called the "all others" bunch which make up a tiny percentage in the overall scheme of things.

I am a dog person. I do not say that with smug pride or arrogance, I say it only as a fact. I am indeed a dog person. I have observed many traits that run consistent among each group of pet owners. It's a well documented fact that pets and owners share common traits. These traits are verifiable and thus validate my three person-stereotype-theory. If you are not a dog person, I've probably already lost you. At least hear me out before you brand me and extremist, dogmatic (pun intended) snob.

First, let's define dog. A real dog can eat a farm animal or at least make a farm animal soil itself in fear. Any animal whose bark truly is worse than its' bite doesn't count. That goes for any animal who should be named Pookie,

Fluffie, FiFi, Snookums or Peaches as well. These actually fall into the "Cat" pet category as their owners share similar traits. Recognizing animal traits will give you great insight into the personalities of the animal's owner. Dogs, for instance, are loyal, honest and trusting. When your best friend runs off with your wife, old Duke is still there for you. No matter what you have done, those big old eyes still hold you in the highest esteem and that tail still wags. That is loyalty. Dogs come to you, you don't have to go looking for them only to have them brush past you in defiant arrogance en route to a table leg to rub against. You can even kick a dog and he will still come back to you. I should point out here that any animal that we have defined as—one who can eat a farm animal—is not an animal that you want to kick. And dogs are honest. Now how can a dog be honest you say? I'm glad you asked, let me start by showing you how sneaky and dishonest cats are. You can draw your own conclusions about what this says about their owners.

There I am one summer afternoon at a friend's house enjoying B.B.Q. Our host proudly shows us the latest recreational addition he has made to his yard. There it is, a full-fledged, regulation, genuine horseshoe pit. Now I don't want to brag too much about my friends, but this was the epitome of horseshoe equipment. The boxes were framed in treated lumber and filled in with real beach sand, the poles were driven in and reinforced. The entire shooting match was set up under an ancient oak tree providing both ambiance and shade. Like I said, they had the works. I get up for my turn to throw and decide to shed my shoes so that I can really enjoy the fresh beach sand. I wiggle my little piggies in that cool sand and, much to my surprise, (not to mention the surprise of the little piggy who had roast beef and the little piggy who had none) a cool, sticky substance oozes up between my toes. Now I grew up playing barefoot in cow pastures and I've got a pretty good idea what that feeling is. And, in the absence of cattle, I can only assume that "Prissy" the cat had made a poo-poo. Dogs are not sneaky, when a dog has to poop, he poops. Big old piles of poop for the entire world to admire. They poop with pride. Cats, on the other hand, are sneaky and hide their mess as if to say, "That smell is not me, I don't know what you are talking about". A dog makes his mess and then runs over to you for approval. That's just pure honesty. Now, all of you cat folks are saying, "Cats are just really clean, he was just covering up his mess". That's not cleanliness, it's deception. And so, dogs are more honest than cats, I rest my case.

I once thought I had made my cat judgement prematurely. I went to a friend's house and he introduces me to his feline companion. This huge, stripped tom comes up and rubs against my leg. My buddy says that he never comes to strangers but seems to have taken to me. I modestly explain that I am at one with the animal world and that they could usually sense that. I scratch Mr. Tomcat between the ears and he purrs like a chainsaw at high idle. I start thinking that maybe cats are not so bad, I mean this one recognizes my oneness with the animal kingdom and has chosen me to share his kitty affection. He's obviously a good judge of character. Suddenly, he takes off and shares his kitty affection with a table leg, a high backed chair and a stoneware planter. Then, some inner ear emergency siren goes off and he realizes that he is desperately needed in another room. Poof, he's gone. It was at this moment that I realized that cats are schizophrenic. I left my buddy and his mentally ill cat a couple of hours later only to smell the distinctive odor of cat urine on my truck seat. My buddy thinks that is cute. That should tell you something about cat people, you can't even leave your window open around a cat. Like I said, cats are just plain sneaky.

Little dogs are nearly as annoying as cats but nowhere close to reaching the annoyance level of their owners. I have yet to meet the little dog owner who didn't proudly proclaim the unsurpassed bravery and tenacity of their little guardian. "Bitsy is absolutely ferocious", I heard one woman say, "She snarls fiercely if anyone comes near me". The she shows me a picture of a hairless rat with a thyroid condition and says, "Isn't she adorable?". That was not the word I was looking for.

That whole picture thing is another cat/little dog trait. While grandmothers are breaking out pictures of their adorable little grandchildren, cat people are flashing photos of "Fluffy" and expect you to swoon over it like it's the cutest thing since the Gerber baby. How much can you say about a cat? "Yep, that sure is a cat", is about all I can muster. You can throw in "fuzzy" or something but it's hard to round up much enthusiasm about a cat or midget mutt. I actually saw a lady carrying her dog when they went for a walk. I'm wondering who is the trained animal? Another thing about cat and little dog owners is that always proclaim, with smug satisfaction, how picky their pet is. "Foofi would never eat that", a cat owner once told me. "He requires the gourmet (translation = expensive) brand of food". I'm thinking that this is a cat that has never been truly hungry or he'd be munching down on some generic cat chow and be happy to have it. Come on now, God made cats to eat rodents. It's only stupid pet owners that let them get picky. Compared to a couple of rats, cheap cat food should look like a filet mignon. In my extremely narrow view of cats, once a cat loses the ability to catch and eat mice, it loses its' purpose for existence. I should probably make this the last chapter so that cat people don't stop reading here, but since most cat people consider themselves superior anyway, they will probably think that I hold these opinions because I am ignorant and will pity me instead of being angry. At least, that is the theory, I haven't tested it yet. I will have to get back to you with the results.

One last trait that I'd like to share with you about cat people is that they have absolutely no sense of humor. A co-worker of mine told me that she often brushed her cat's teeth. The amazed look on my face prompted her to explain that brushing kept her cat's breath from smelling bad. I told her that my dog's breath never smelled bad. She wondered aloud at what miracle of pet dentistry could keep a dog's breath from smelling. I told her that I poured Listerine on all of the neighborhood cats. I laughed, she cried; it was only a joke. Besides, everyone knows that Scope smells better than Listerine.

Now let's look for a moment at the last group. It's kind of like "d" on a multiple choice test for "all others". I call it a minor group only because of it's relatively small numbers and not because of it's significance. These include owners of snakes, mice, iguanas, spiders, ferrets and weasels. These folks are pretty much normal except that they seem kind of eerie from time to time. This group also include the "no pets" bunch. This group would ordinarily be normal except that most of them have had some kind of bad pet experience as children and have never recovered. Goldfish would probably be good therapy for these people. Goldfish die way before you get attached to or tired of them. You can always flush them without too much drama as well. Despite having extreme pets, most people in the "all others" group aren't nearly as extreme as their dog and cat owner counterparts. You don't usually see, "I Love My Iguana" bumper stickers or, "Tarantula on Board" signs in the rearview window like you do with dog and cat owners. The "all others" bunch is a more reserved, though slightly rebellious group who don't try to impose their pet beliefs off on you. They're a pretty good bunch for the most part, and except for having snakes come out of their shirts from time to time, they are not too bad to be around. As for me, give me a big dog and a big pooper scooper and all is well with the world. Don't forget to watch where you step.

RANSOM PHILLIPS

Ransom Phillips was a friend of mine. He was half of a century older and a whole world wiser than me. He had been most everywhere and done most everything and had every detail permanently etched in his razor sharp memory. One of my roommates in college was his grandson. We visited him most Friday nights and went fishing with him most Saturday mornings. Ransom was what we in the South call a "Good Old Boy". In the hierarchy of redneck status symbols, "Good Old Boy" is the highest possible honor one can hope to achieve. A Good Old Boy is never called that in his presence, he would be far too modest for that kind of showy emotion. In fact, the honor is usually bestowed posthumously when old men in overalls sit around the feed store and talk of long past hunting buddies. He is the man who gets up first in deer camp to make coffee, he votes because he knows it's a privilege not afforded elsewhere, he works hard because that is the right thing to do and he never looks for a handout but is the first to offer his hand to someone in need. He always tells the truth unless it's a fishing story and then he only stretches the truth a little bit. A Good Old Boy is what men strived to be back when being a man meant something more than which restroom he used. Ransom Phillips was a Good Old Boy.

Despite the fact that a well equipped bass boat was readily available, he always sat on the bank on an old metal bucket full of treble hooks and chicken livers when we went fishing. He always carried a box of Little Debbie snack cakes and white label, generic cigarettes. Many spring sunrises found Ransom on the banks of a lake, fly rod in hand. I never knew why he used a fly rod, but watching him catch a ten pound catfish with it was quality entertainment and the story telling opportunities were almost limitless. I'd sit next to him, with my complete arsenal of the latest hi-tech fishing equipment and watch him land fish after fish, all the while laughing at me. With a little encouragement, Ransom would start on a story of long ago and far away and entertain me for hours. I didn't catch many fish but I learned far more on the banks of those rivers and lakes in Southern Arkansas than I ever learned in any college classroom. For some reason, know only to him, Ransom never called me by my name, only "Boy".

My roommates and I would show up at his house on a Friday night, bound for some fishing or camping adventure. We'd find Ransom sitting in his favorite old chair, complete with loose armrests and exposed springs, watching the Atlanta Braves (and usually cussing the Braves). "Hello boy", he'd say to me as he crushed out a cigarette. "Evening Ransom", I'd reply. Ransom wasn't much on lengthy conversation during Braves games. "You boys going camping tonight? Build a good fire, it's gonna be colder than a #%@&* tonight" he would advise. It didn't matter what time of year it was, he always had the same advice. We'd watch a couple of innings, he'd cuss in disgust, and then we would head out to wherever we were going, again reminded to build a good fire. He always asked us later how our adventures went and we would give him a complete play by play which would usually remind him of a story. I've always wondered who enjoyed the stories more, us or him.

After a couple of years in the Navy, I went back to see Ransom. Those generic cigarettes took him a few months before I got there. I never really got to say goodbye to Ransom, but then he wasn't much for mushy goodbyes either. It would be a lie if I said that I didn't love that old man. But much more than love him, I respected him and in the time from which he came, that meant a whole lot more. After all, Ransom Phillips was a Good Old Boy.

PEANUT BUTTER AND JELLY

Every person has something that ignites their passion. It may be the love of a beautiful woman, money, a career or even a sport. Mine is simple; I love food. Yes, I love to eat. I like to talk about food, think about food, and cook food. Most of all, I like to eat food. I like to talk about food while I'm eating and eat food while I'm talking. All in all, I love food.

I come from a family of big eaters which means that I come from a family of big people. We like to think of ourselves as fluffy, not fat. Unfortunately, Uncle Sam views obesity as a bad thing. So, in order to stay within the Navy's regulations on what a physically fit person should look like, I went on a diet. Keep in mind that I have always viewed diets and diet foods as being for people who don't have the courage to enjoy being fat. I have always had that courage but Uncle Sam decided otherwise for me. My wife, who has the excess body fat of a mosquito, and I decided that it was time to lose weight. She said that she was up three pounds and that it was driving her crazy. Being an Olympic class eater, I told her that three pounds was little more than a good snack. But we dieted anyway. First, we started with the powder stuff. At first, it wasn't too bad. I came home from work with an open mind and sat down to a healthy meal of salad and the powder stuff. I sucked down both in anxious anticipation of the main meal. I sat and sat but there was no main meal. I was determined not to panic so I casually asked my wife what was the main course. She informed me that I had eaten the main course. She goes on to explain that the salad and crushed chalk dust had all of the ingredients that my chubby little body needed to survive. Not so I tell her, I had yet to eat meat. There was no meat she said.

Prior to this point, I had always considered my wife to be a fairly intelligent person. I was amazed that I had to explain the facts of life as they relate to food. I pointed out that seventy-five percent of the word meat was contained in the word meal. Obviously, that meant that meat should comprise seventy-five percent of a meal. I thought this was a generally accepted fact. She had never heard of that theory but I straightened her out. Man is omnivorous I explained. That means that he eats everything and that he hasn't eaten anything until there is a dead animal somewhere on the plate. A meal should be a pleasurable experience, something to be relished and savored, not a punishment.

Then I joined the Navy. Navy food is like no other food on Earth. It doesn't look, smell or taste like anything you've ever seen. You don't try to identify it, you just choke it down. In order to eat Navy food, you have to change your outlook on the purpose for eating. Eating for me had always been for the purpose of satisfying not only my hunger, but each of my other five senses as well. I took great pleasure in the sight, smell, taste and touch of food and nothing thrilled my heart more than to hear that frying pan sizzling in the kitchen. The Navy destroyed that. A Navy meal serves only to push the preceding meal through your system. It is a very mechanical act that requires no thought, no taste, no smell, just chewing. It is much easier to think of catsup as cover-up. After a few of these unique experiences, I soon learned to turn off all of my senses and just eat. I learned to expect nothing and be disappointed in nothing. Occasionally, something would come across the chow line that I recognized sparking a brief moment of hope.

One quick bite killed off that hope and kept it from becoming a recurring feeling. I soon learned that just because something looked like my wife's cooking, didn't mean that it tasted like my wife's cooking.

The Navy is perfect for young, married couples in that respect. After a couple of months on a ship, even the worst cook looks like a star pupil of the Cordon Bleu. Young sailors soon learn to praise their wife's cooking attempts and get pretty good at making peanut butter and jelly sandwiches. After only two short years in the Navy, I had raised sandwich making to an art form. One quick look at me now and you will realize that my wife still is a wonderful cook, and, to her credit, I haven't had a peanut butter and jelly sandwich in years.

The primary reason that the Navy can get away with having lousy food is that when a ship goes underway, most of the picky people are too sick to eat anyway. Nothing cures a healthy appetite like being seasick. Been there, done that. There are many humiliating experiences, but few can compare to heaving your guts out in some foreign body of water in front of your co-workers. I've seen some pretty tough guys get sick, and it's not a pretty sight. There is usually some helpful person smoking cheap cigars and eating smoked oysters in front of you to help you get that sick feeling out of your stomach and into the garbage can. The cooks always managed to have greasy chili on the day that we got underway. If not chili, then chili-mac. That is the most disgusting combination of incongruent ingredients imaginable. Macaroni with chili thrown in there for good measure. It looks like a really ugly accident involving a tractor trailer full of machetes and a herd of goats.

These distasteful meals made trips to the head (restroom) terribly unpleasant. Not everyone was an expert in projectile vomiting like I was. During an excursion to the North Atlantic, I had the misfortune of combining seasickness with chili-mac. The two made a lovely combination that had me begging for someone who really loved me to shoot me and put me out of my misery. I could find no such person. I was camped out in my rack, lamenting my pitiful condition, and praying that relief or death would soon come. The door to the head was directly across from my rack and had a well worn path between the two. Mine was not the only path that was well worn.

My stomach then decided that it was time to purge but I tried to lay perfectly still in hopes that it would soon pass. It did not soon pass. I then shifted my attention to postponing the inevitable so that I might go between swells. Suddenly, my other end decided that postponement was not a viable option. And so I sprinted, setting a new indoor speed record which was later disallowed because it was wave aided. I burst into the head in search of relief. There were four stalls and I opened the first only to find a long lost shipmate holding onto the toilet for dear life. The next stall revealed a person in a similar condition as the first who didn't appear to want to share. The third door was locked and the final door held behind it a man with his face pressed against the cool porcelain toilet. Life had suddenly taken a cruel turn and didn't appear willing to relent. My last hope was a deep sink just across from the last toilet. I should stop here and explain a few things about gravity drains and moving ships. Water runs downhill, in a stationary building, downhill remains in the same direction. On a ship that rocks and rolls in the waves, downhill sometimes changes directions and thus, objects in those gravity drains change direction as well. That being said, I grabbed the sink with reckless abandon and hung my head down in the sink in preparation to purge. I learned a wonderful purge technique but I won't go into too much detail here because it is fairly disgusting, but suffice it to say that I had it down pat. Just as lunch was appearing from the depths of my stomach, a piece of human waste bubbled up from the drain into the couple of inches of water in the bottom of the deep sink. I screamed which was barely audible over the sound of the vomit. I then vomited which was barely audible over the sound of my screaming and so on and so on.

That was the worst of my experiences with Navy food and Navy plumbing. I never forgot it and still get queasy when I see chili or macaroni.

AN AMERICAN HERO

Gordon Fist is an American hero. You don't know his name and have never seen his face on a stamp or even a memorial. In fact, other than what I tell you, you won't know anything about him. First of all, he was a kid (all of 24 years old) from Carolina. He died for his country in the Persian Gulf. He served his country in the most un-American job possible, the military. Now before you call your local VFW, hear me out. The military voluntarily forfeits fundamental rights in order to protect the rights of others. There is no freedom of speech, you can't go where you want to when you want to, and you opinion definitely does not count. That is un-American and worse yet, the pay is horrible. So why do it?

I pondered all these questions in the toilet. I was not using it; I was cleaning it. The answer came pretty clearly to me. Having visited with those who never tasted freedom, the preservation and spreading of that freedom brings to life words like duty, honor and courage. You learn to cherish things that you took for granted before. Yes, it's mushy, but I love my country. I paid not for my freedom, but for the freedom of my children and their children. Just as those men and women who went before me paid for my freedom. I'm proud of the time I spent in service of my country and proud that I knew a man like Gordon. I owe a great debt to him and to all of those who went before him. He is a hero. I know that you have never heard of him before now, but his mother and father lost a son, grandparents lost a grandson, girlfriend lost a boyfriend, shipmates lost a friend and his country lost one of it's hero's. He, and men and women like him, work hard for you to enjoy the privileges that you now enjoy. Even now, as you read this, a service member is standing watch somewhere, whether home or abroad, and is ready to die so that you may have the right to burn the very flag that he serves and will one day cover his casket.

I have now stepped down from my soapbox but will keep it handy just in case. I make no apologies for my shameless patriotism. It's not politically correct, but you can probably conclude my opinion of PC. So, the next time that you assemble in public, pray to your God, or complain about your elected officials, remember to say "Thank you" to those who afforded you those rights. God bless the U.S.A.

RAISE YOUR HAND

Each family has it's own traditions and rituals that are unique to that family. These traditions may be centered around holiday festivities, birthdays or even ordinary events. Our family has such a tradition. It all started quite innocently while I was working in the oilfield as a mechanic's helper. One of my primary duties was to drain and change the oil in the compressors and engines that we serviced. Being a mechanical idiot, I was often misunderstood by my mechanically gifted employer who acted as though no one had ever accidentally drained the radiator instead of the engine. He suggested that I should admit my own mistake by raising my hand, stating my name, and saying, "I am a moron" (pronounced "MO—RON" in two separate words). This would save my boss the trouble of having to tell me that I am a moron.

Thus, a tradition was born. A tradition driven by honor and duty. In our family, it is one's moral duty to report their own foolish actions by simply raising a hand and saying, "My name is Budd; I am a Mo—Ron". While this tradition was created for me, it soon spread to my family and friends. I never fully realized the scope of its growth until one day while working in the shop with the creator of my now famous tradition. My employer was prying a piece of metal keystock out of a shaft with a screwdriver. Normally, those keys pop right out, but this one was feeling especially obstinate. A shift in weight to produce more leverage had the desired effect and the metal key popped free followed shortly by a hollow thud sound, not unlike thumping a ripe watermelon. Normally, I am a very compassionate man, but the sight of my boss grasping for the little stars that were dancing before his eyes coupled with the crescent moon shaped indentation squarely centered on his forehead robbed me of my composure and forced me to scream with laughter. As soon as I realized how career-threatening my laughter was, I managed to hold it down with a minimum of stomach trembling and lip biting. I lost it once again when I saw my boss' hand rise in the air as he confessed, "My name is Tim and I am a Mo-Ron".

The devious among you are probably wondering why one would profess their own blunder and not simply try to hide it. Those of you thinking this way, and you know who you are, are probably cat owners. As I stated before, this is a tradition born of honor, duty and moral integrity. Besides, the humiliation is nothing compared with trying to hide it and getting caught. This has never happened to me personally unless you count the knife in the leg incident, but I really don't have time to go into that right now.

My wife became somewhat of an unwilling participant in this tradition during baseball season one year. She, of the quick to point out your mistake variety, was not so quick to share her blunder with the rest of us. As a diehard St. Louis Cardinals fan, she was watching a game against my beloved Houston Astros. Ozzie Smith, the longtime Cardinals superhero shortstop, made of his patented diving catches to end the inning. Using the inning change for a restroom break, I got up to leave the room. My wife was discussing something with me that I may or may not have been paying attention to when she turned back towards the television and excitedly yelled, "Honey, you're not going to believe this but Ozzie just made another great catch exactly like the last one". I put my arm around her to calm her down and lovingly pointed out the modern miracle of instant replay. Of course, this would require the Mo-Ron statement which she said was unfair because she had been distracted by our conversation. However, after appealing it to the official rules committee, it was ruled that this was, in fact, an official Mo-Ron moment.

The beauty of the Mo-Ron moment is its innocence. It is self—proclaimed so it is not cruel and all of the joking is done at one's own expense. It usually doesn't involve anyone else so no one else is affected. The notable exception to this rule took place in the Big Horn National Park near Buffalo, Wyoming. My pastor, who has been a longtime hunting buddy, domino partner, fishing companion and full time friend and I were on a once-in-a-lifetime elk hunt in the mountains. Both from South Texas, we were completely in awe of the majestic beauty of the mountains. The aspen has turned golden and the hearty pines were wrapped in a white blanket of snow as if to protect them from the coming winter. We stopped just to drink in the glory of all of God's handiwork, each trying to commit the scene to memory so that we could recall it in the coming oppressive heat of the South Texas summer. Snow bunnies played in the soft snow while as squirrels scurried to gather last minute winter supplies. We were both drawn into ourselves and individually enjoying the moment of serenity. This was my very own Eutopia. My golden euphoria was shattered as I was dragged from my temporary trance by the motion of a solitary hand shooting high in the mountain air and the quiet confession, "My name is Harold, I am a Mo-Ron". The question that must have been evident on my face was answered with one nod towards the truck where I could clearly see the keys hanging from the ignition and the doors securely locked.

MY LITTLE MAN

There are certain rites of passage into manhood that marks a young man's entry into the next level of social male development. Some cultures pierce or tattoo various body parts, others marry, others move out on their own. In our small corner of South Texas, manhood is often marked in terms of first hunts and first game killed. While this may sound barbaric to the more sensitive readers, there should be some comfort in the knowledge that more game animals have died from laughter at my expense than from my marksmanship.

Dove hunting is a popular sport here and I dreamed of the day when my first born, my manchild, would accompany me, not as a spectator but as a hunting partner. I have to admit that I was sad to lose the finest retriever I had ever had, not only could the boy retrieve, he was good company and carried the extra shells. Still, I was proud when we set out one fine evening in September with my faithful shotgun, my son, and his shotgun (the same one that I used twenty years earlier). This is also a rite of passage for a father and I was just slightly less excited than my son. I gave him my best safety lecture, the same one I heard from my father, and he gave me the same "one hundred times is enough, Dad" look that I gave my dad a couple of decades earlier. We settled into a fence line just behind a small pond where the doves would be coming just before dark. The birds flew and my boy shot, and shot and shot. Each miss brought a look of disappointment to his face and the ching-ching sound of a cash register to my ears (those .410 shells are very expensive). My son's disappointment was growing at the same rate that his enjoyment of dove hunting was slipping away. I gave him my best pep talk and he gave me a brave smile but I could tell he wasn't convinced.

About that time, a group of three birds came in towards us over the pond. We both shot and one of the birds fell a dozen or so yards from me. My son looked dejected as he watched the other two birds fly off in the other direction. "Come here, Brett", I yelled his way. "There's a bird down over here you need to get". "I missed him, Dad", he said. "Well, I saw one fall and I need some help finding him", I replied. Doubtful, he headed where I was pointing. Within seconds he looked back at me with the missing-tooth grin reaching both ears. He reached down and picked up his prize and proudly exclaimed, "I bet those birds won't try to fly over me any more". No, I bet they won't. We both made it through another step in our male development. My son had his first bird and I had the chance to share it with him. We didn't pierce or tattoo any body parts but it seemed to me that my son turned into a little man before my very eyes.

TRAYCE AND AN ANGUS

On another such hunting expedition, I was sitting on my trusty old camouflaged stool, absorbing the subtle beauty of my surroundings. The harsh glare of the September sun had reluctantly given way to a soft, warm, amber glow that made everything it descended upon look like a scene from a time long ago. The ancient, wooden windmill slowly turning in the gentle breeze, standing watch like a lone sentinel over the mesquite trees as the mystical glow from the fading sun fell on them on it's silent journey into the western landscape. The birds and the insects hushed their busy noises and watched the same scene that had me entranced.

It was in that very moment of serenity that I saw him, Trayce, my youngest son. He was to the be completion of our perfect, American dream family. After five years of trying, it looked like we would never have another child. A long succession of doctors told us that we were to be a family of three and no more. We had all but given up when my wife announced that she was, in fact, with child. Our prayers were answered and our dreams had come true. Life was perfect until the second day after his birth when we were told that Trayce had holes in his heart. The doctors explained that this was serious but not uncommon and so we prayed. We prayed that we would have a healthy and happy child that would run and play like other little children.

Over the next several months, our baby was diagnosed with muscular dystrophy, multiple sclerosis, cerebral palsy and numerous other maladies that I can't pronounce and won't even attempt to spell. Each time a new ailment was suggested as his problem, we prayed. We prayed that he would be a healthy and happy baby that would run and play like other little children. Each time we seemed to find no answer to our prayers.

Every specialist offered his or her opinion as to the cause of his aliment, but none offered a solution or even hope. And still we prayed. God reminded me of my prayers on the hunting trip as I looked across the pasture in horror to see my three year old not two feet from a full grown angus cow. As I desperately scrambled across the pasture toward my child, I could hear him yell (he always yells) "HELL-OOO, HOW ARE YOU? I AM FINE, THANK—YOU!". And, indeed he was fine, a healthy and happy little boy that runs and plays like all the other little children. And, on occasion, he even talks to cows. Thank you, God.

THE SUPERMARKET INCIDENT

In our small town, there is a well known food store chain which supplies nearly all of your shopping needs. Short of tires and a lube job, you can get just about everything else that you need in just one stop. They have the latest in everything. They have a flower shop, bakery, pizza oven and you can even grind your own coffee. They also have a bulletin board with pictures of my family on it with a note in big letters underneath it with words to the effect that we are to be shot on sight and then call the manager. O.K., they won't really shoot at us. I think the manager was kidding when he said that.

It started pretty innocently when my wife ran to town to pick up a few groceries ($200.00 worth) one evening. The trip was pretty uneventful until the checkout began. My middle child, of cow yelling fame, noticed that there were plugs on the post leading to the checkout computer. Now in the old days, a cashier rang you up on an old fashioned cash register that chinged with each sale and then a drawer popped out to receive your money. It was a quaint experience that seemed to work fine until some computer weenie came up with the idea of computerizing the process. But, this new computer needs electricity to feed it and thus is required to be plugged in. My son took note of this shortcoming and decided to investigate the plug. It occurred to my young son that he could look at the plug much closer if it were in his hand so he yanked it out of the socket. This experience brought him so much pleasure that he pulled the other plug out of the socket. I think it was the flickering lights that alerted someone that there was a problem, or it may have been all of the screens going blank. At any rate, it was probably one of those two things that got someone's attention and soon the young assistant manager came a-runnin.

Naturally, the customers at all thirty check-out counters were a little put out, but the young assistant manager assured all concerned that everything would be fine in a matter of minutes. And it was a matter of minutes, after the manager and computer weenie showed up from home, it was a matter of forty-five minutes to be exact. I don't think the manager was very upset about my boy shutting down the entire store, and I really don't think he was all that upset about having all of his customers waiting around for nearly an hour, but I do think that having his entire inventory erased from the store's computer was the final straw that made him full-fledged, eye-twitching, lip-quivering mad. By the time the computer weenie had re-booted the program and got everything up and running again, the manager had managed to calm down and stop screaming. In a measured and deliberate voice, the manager asked incredulously, "how could this happen?". "Easy", Trayce replied, "just like this", as he demonstrated his technique and then handed the plug to the store manager. That was probably when he got the idea for the sign with our pictures on it and the directions to shoot on sight.

I like to frequent a store on the other side of town run by an elderly couple who are the only employees. The old man tells me war stories and his wife always sends home a piece of candy for the kids. It's shopping the way shopping used to be. You can't get everything there but they have a whole lot of things that you can't find in the new stores, like a genuine ching-ching cash register. There are also some noticeable items missing, like my family's picture on the wall with instructions underneath that are less that shopper friendly.

RAID, ANTS AND THE SMOKING SCREWDRIVER

Some stories beg to be told, some stories beg to be forgotten. Common sense would dictate that this story would be forgotten, but I have a remarkable lack of common sense. It would be much funnier if it were about someone else, it's not. Our first house in Texas was what could be best described as a farm house in a hayfield. Our landlord refurbished some old houses and stuck them in the middle of a prairie and that was home. What makes a fine hayfield does not necessarily make a good place to live. All the new roads around the flat hayfield made it hold water like a bowl. A one inch rain brought ankle deep water and knee deep critters. It would seem that animals of all sort move to higher ground when it floods. We were higher ground. Ants, snakes, lizards, field mice and kangaroo rats sought out and found our house.

One Saturday with enough sunshine to allow me to mow, I mowed, weeded and poisoned. After a hard day's work, a man needs a shower and I mean he really needs a shower. And so I turned on the water and was just about ready to get in when I heard a scream. We are talking about a world class, bleached-blonde in a "B" movie who finds her boyfriend's head in the refrigerator kind of scream. I ran out of the bathroom and grabbed my shotgun from the bedroom. Now I am naked, but very well armed. A quick survey of the living rooms revealed no bad guys, evil doers or anything of the like, just my wife staring out of the window and screaming. I looked out of the window at nothing in particular and finally had to ask her what was wrong. "There's millions of them", she screams. "Millions of what?" I asked. "They're coming from everywhere", she stammers nearly in hysterics. Then I saw the reason for her panic. Coming from the wall socket under the window were thousands of fire ants.

"People will think we are dirty", she cried. I assure her that no one will think poorly of her housekeeping and moved closer to assess the damage. She disappeared and the general chaos seemed to die down. I inspected the wall socket beneath the window unit at the trail of tiny invaders and tried to decide my best course of action. About that time, my wife reappeared with the industrial strength Raid and began dousing the wall. It has never occurred to my wife that the poison will kill the ants. She thinks that the liquid will just drown them, at least that is the way that it looked to me. I tried to point out that spraying a liquid stream into a 220 volt socket is probably not a wise move. Undaunted, she kept on spraying with reckless abandon. I finally managed to wrestle the can away from her and get the situation somewhat under control.

Our house had hardwood floors throughout the house. My wife kept them shining so that you could see yourself in them which is what reminded me that I was still quite naked when I bent down to inspect the poison drenched socket. I won't go into great detail at this point, but trust me, it really wouldn't add much to the story. I then went into my junk drawer to find just the tool that I needed for this special emergency. Fortunately, I had a brass screwdriver for just such occasions. I removed the cover plate of the wall socket only to find thousands upon thousands of ants crammed into the tiny space. It was quite a sight. It reminded me of the time they had dollar day at Kendall's department store and all of those lady shoppers crammed in there causing a small riot. That was the scene in my wall socket. I figured my brass screwdriver made me nearly invincible and that I could dig some of those ants out before any serious damage was done.

Then I saw the bright light. It was a warm and gentle light. I wanted to go to it. I could hear laughter in the distance. This was truly a happy place. I thought for a moment that I was in Heaven until I felt something shaking me. It grew rougher and rougher until I opened my eyes. When I did, I saw my wife standing over me. Oh good, I though, my wife is in Heaven with me. There was a smile on her face even as she was shaking me. "Are you alright?", she asked. "Yes, never better, why do you ask?" I replied. Then she started laughing again and left me to figure out the details.

As near as I can tell, all of those ants were wet from the dousing that my wife gave them and must have been in contact with the live wires in the socket. Apparently, wet ants conduct electricity. That would explain the smoking screwdriver in my hand with the melted tip. I'm not sure how far the jolt threw me, but the skid marks on my naked behind suggest that it was quite a ways. As for the laughing, I can only hope that it was a laugh from hysteria rather than the sight of me laying naked on the floor with a smoking screwdriver in my hand. I can only guess as to what actually killed the ants. It was either the poison or they indeed drowned as I had suspected. Their little charred bodies made it difficult to determine cause of death.

THE BALLAD OF DOC

Doc was comical in almost every way. Skinny, freckle faced with pants pulled up to just below his armpits and large glasses that magnified his eyes and made him look like an owl; Doc was my left fielder. Quite possibly the smartest nine year old that ever lived, Doc had an opinion on just about any subject from horse breeding to weapons and he was never bashful about sharing those opinions. Just before our first baseball game of the season, I gathered the team around for a pep talk. I asked if anyone knew who we were playing that day and Doc's hand shot up; it always shot up. "Coach, we are playing the worst beef producing cattle in the State of Texas", he said followed by, "I think they have an internal parasite problem". "Yes", I replied, "but they couldn't get all of that on the T-shirt so they just went with 'Longhorns'". He seemed satisfied with that answer.

He showed up one day to practice wearing about a fifty-gallon cowboy hat on his two-gallon head. The ensemble was complete with twin six shooters with imitation pearl handles and plastic holster. He announced that he wouldn't be able to make practice that day because he had a prior engagement. Afraid to risk the wrath of the twin six guns, I just said that would be fine. He tipped his hat and strolled off into the sunset. I am pretty sure that he had planned that walking into the sunset thing. After a called third strike, he decided that an umpire who would have the audacity to make such a call should be dealt with severely. I asked what he had in mind and he said he thought he could slip some diesel into the umpire's water bottle and then offer him a cigarette. By this time, I was no longer shocked by any of Doc's plans especially after the entire frog-branding episode. I just did my best to steer him away from any talk of planned homicide or weapons of mass destruction. Aside from that, he was a pretty normal kid.

Doc had plenty of advice for a novice coach such as myself. He chastised me for putting him in right field and promptly informed me that right field would, undoubtedly, throw his equilibrium out of sync since he had never played on that side of the field. I assured him that he would be fine but I don't think I ever truly convinced him. Every team meeting started with and ended with a litany of questions from Doc. Some relating to baseball (usually the fact that I was overlooking his obvious pitching talent), most relating to whatever was on his mind at the time. Every time his hand shot up in the air, I halfway enjoyed the anticipation of what he would come up with and halfway dreaded him asking a question that I had no answer to.

And so it was at that Monday afternoon practice when his hand shot up, I was completely filled with dread. We had a game the Saturday before that we had to cancel. We cancelled because on the way to the game, one of our players had been badly injured along with his brother. Less fortunate than her boys, their mother had lost her life. I had spent the day before in the hospital visiting those two boys who had just lost their mother and with their grandmother who had just lost her daughter. I had spoken to each parent and knew that I had to tell the boys something, problem was, I didn't know what that "something" was. Some of the parents had confided that they hadn't told their boys anything and weren't sure what to tell them. I knew that when they got to school on Monday, everyone would know. News travels fast in a small town, especially bad news. I remember when I was that age and anytime something bad would happen the kids were always left out. I didn't want to do that to my boys. I wanted them to know that I trusted them enough to share news even if it was bad news. I spent all day Monday trying to decide what to tell them. I promised myself that I wasn't going to cry in front of a bunch of nine and ten year old boys, I wanted to be strong for them. I gave them the best speech that I could. I told them what had happened and reminded them that I had always told them that we were more than a team, we were a family and families take care of each other. I told them that their teammate would not be allowed to play the rest of that year due to his injuries but that he was still part of our team. I said that maybe he could sit on the bench with the rest of the team. I then told them that sometimes when something bad happens to a friend, you don't know what to say so you end up not saying anything. I didn't want that to happen to them. I wanted them to let their friend know that he was still part of our team. Sometimes being there is more important than saying anything I reminded them. Before I could go any farther, Doc's hand shot up in the air. Before I could even ask him what he wanted, he blurted out, "Coach, if he comes back, I don't want to play". "You don't?" I was amazed.

"No sir, I just want to sit on the bench next to him so that he will know that I am his friend".

As a little boy, I was taught that cowboys don't suck their thumbs and they don't cry. Bound and determined not to cry in front of a bunch of little boys, I turned my back. At least I didn't suck my thumb.

SCREEN DOORS AND OTHER RAMBLINGS

Creeeeek, Slam!! The screen door shut just inches behind a little boy running out of the door. In the background his Momma could be heard yelling, "In or out, I'm not air conditioning the whole neighborhood" or, the ever popular, "You're letting flies in". And such was life in the South in the 70's and probably for the hundred years prior to that, minus the "Air Conditioning" statement. The air was hot, thick, humid, and mosquito infested. The A/C sent out a blast of arctic ice wind that could cool off even the hottest little soldier or commando or whoever you happened to be that day. If you sat in front of it too long, you were liable to catch your death of pneumonia (it must have been true because my Momma said so) and then have to get a shot.

Some time during the first half of the 70's, a new invention came to our household; central air conditioning. I knew from experience that an A/C unit could only cool the room that it was in and then, only if you kept the door shut. So, I wasn't too sure how this "central" thing was going to work because the machine wasn't even in the house at all. In fact, it was on the far side of the garage. I didn't want to say anything to my dad but I really couldn't understand why he would want to cool the garage. Dad always seemed to know what he was doing so I figured that he had a plan for this too. Before long, that machine was singing out a gentle "Whuuuuuur" sound. Standing there, I couldn't feel any cool air so I leaned over it and sure enough, air was blowing out. The only problem was, it was hot air. I knew better than to say, "I told you so", but I was feeling pretty smug about myself. The only thing was, we had already gotten rid of those window units so I figured it was going to be hot that night.

Much to my surprise, when I walked into the house I was greeted by cold air. I didn't know how he did it, but Dad was right all along. Things kind of changed after that. The screen door was replaced with a glass one (that you couldn't put your hands on because it left fingers prints) that we were warned about a gazillion times not to slam that door because it would break. Along about then, I learned that air could get out. Momma would say, "Close that door, you're letting all the air out". I didn't know how much air there was but I figured that "central" machine was making it and if it all ran out, everyone would know. I would hurry in and out of the door and shut it behind me (without slamming it of course). I knew Momma was right because when I shut the door, I could feel the cool air coming with me. I didn't know how she knew it, but she knew it. I had this hidden fear that I would leave the door open on accident and she would come in and all of the air would be gone. Of course she would know that it was me that did it, it was always me that did it.

One day my worst fears came true. My brother and I were flying kites, which is normally a fairly harmless adventure for children. But not for us, oh no, we spiced it up by shooting them down with B-B guns. Now that was adventure. I should probably make it clear here that it really wasn't all my fault, if my younger brother, Mason, hadn't flown that kite right in front of the window, I never would have shot it. But, as fate would have it, I did shoot it. I would also like to interject that I made a perfect shot and hit the kite dead center. Unfortunately, I hit the window dead center as well. There was a perfectly round little B-B sized hole in the window. When I put my finger up to it, I could feel the air running out. I was doomed. It never occurred to me all of the bad things that could happen if the air ran out. My mother was in the house and I didn't know if she would even have enough air to breathe—we had just learned about breathing air in Science class. Suddenly, I came up with a brilliant idea. I ran to the bathroom to the medicine cabinet (both my brother and I were well acquainted with the medicine cabinet). There were only three items in the medicine cabinet, red stuff we called "Monkey Blood", baby aspirins and Band-Aids. I knew the Band-Aid would do the trick. I took the smallest one in the package and covered the hole with the precision of a well trained surgeon and, Presto, no more air running out.

I learned early on that it was better to have an explanation prepared than to act like something didn't happen. Besides, it was going to be pretty hard to pretend that there wasn't a Band-Aid on the window. So, I devised a story that should be the envy of most any window breaker. About the time that I put the finishing touches on my brilliant story (it revolved around another new invention, the Weedeater), I heard my dad's old Ford pickup truck come rolling up the driveway. I was ready with my story but didn't want to look anxious so I was going to wait and let him discover the window. That way I could act like I had prevented grave injury to my family by preventing all of the air from running of the house. If he didn't discover it for several days, all the better. Of course it wasn't several days. It wasn't even several minutes. When my dad came outside he walked straight to the window. He called me over and asked why there was a hole in the window. I said I didn't know how the hole got there but that I had put the Band-Aid over the hole so all the air wouldn't get out. He wasn't nearly as pleased as I had hoped. "How do you suppose that hole got there?" he asked. I said I wasn't sure but hinted that his new Weedeater might be the culprit. I was just as cool as the other side of the pillow and knew that I was home free. "I've never seen such a tiny, perfectly round hole as that" he answered. "I don't think that could have come from edging" he continued. I really didn't see that one coming but, being quick on my feet, I boldly responded, "Maybe a truck from the highway threw a rock" (Brilliant, huh?). While he was explaining that the highway was too far away to throw a rock that far, he was reaching into his pocket and pulling out a shiny, copper B-B. "Where do you reckon this came from?" he asked. Busted!! After all of the careful planning and slick maneuvering, just plain busted. First figuratively and then literally. Two dollars and seventy-five cents and two whippings (one for shooting out the window and the other for lying), I had paid for my crime and his window. Of course, nothing ever happened to Mason. Did I point out that he is the one who flew the kite in front of the window in the first place? I did, huh?

BEECHNUT

Things were just different back then. Trucks had a vent window. Remember that vent window? It was a little triangular shaped window that let the outside air in without rolling the window down. If there was anything sitting on the dash, it would get blown around and the whining of the wind made a lot of racket but that is a pretty decent trade in Southeast Texas during the summer. Most vehicles didn't come equipped with air conditioning back then, at least not the vehicles that my family owned. It was that little window that gave me my first inspiration to accomplish something monumental.

While riding in the truck with my buddy, his mom and dad (seatbelts, what seatbelts?), my buddy's dad tilted his head slightly and sent a stream of tobacco juice out that little window. It may have been the single greatest feat of physical dexterity that I have ever witnessed. Not one drop on the seat, dash or window. He didn't have a spit cup, didn't roll down the window and didn't spit on the floorboard. I was completely amazed. I knew that one day, I too, would accomplish that feat. Some strive for fame and fortune; I wanted to spit out of the vent window.

After I got my first truck, complete with vent window, I truly began to appreciate what an incredible accomplishment it was to hit that window. My first attempt went down the front of my shirt, nerves I guess. Next try went down the window (wiped that one up with my elbow). I finally gave up and rolled down the window. I practiced for a while with water and thought I had my technique down pat. I really wanted to have it refined to a fine art before I demonstrated it publicly. Back in the saddle again, full of confidence, I splattered a fair amount of juice all over the vent window. Forgot to open the stupid vent window. Then it happened, just like that. Just like I had been doing it all of my life, viola, right out the vent window (I remembered to open it). I joined some cool club that most people didn't even know existed. Yep, I was cool. Sure the inside of my truck was stained brown, but it kind of matched the seat anyway. About that time, another friend of mine blew up the engine in my truck.

My next truck did not have a vent window. That changed the complexion of things. I was now required to roll down the window. Once you have experienced the thrill of great accomplishment, it is extremely difficult to go backwards. It was worse than I imagined. My logic was as follows: if I leaned up towards the dash and spit out, the wind would take the spit back, away from the truck. Sound logic, flawed, but sound. The wind did take the spit; took it and blew it right back in my left ear. It is nearly impossible to put into words how it feels to spit into your own ear. That same act, in a pool hall, honky-tonk, feed store or ball game would be grounds for justifiable homicide. But to do it to yourself, there's not a long list of people to blame. Of course, the guy who blew up your engine comes to mind but, eventually, you have to admit that you did it to yourself. Once at the height of vent spitting, now reduced to the lowly shame of, "I spit in my own ear". I should have tried it with water first.

Eventually, I got my technique down. It seems that if you aim at the bottom, outside corner of your rearview mirror, the wind does take it away from the vehicle. It is important to note here that this only works above about 35 mph depending on outside conditions. Somewhere during this time I decided to move on to a cooler brand of tobacco (as if spitting in your own ear weren't cool enough). My great grandmother had dipped snuff. The snuff wasn't that appealing but the really cool tin that it came in was. It was antique and new wave all at the same time. The tobacco even smelled good. I decided that snuff was for me; it wasn't. I had seen many older people dip snuff, some even sniffed it. I never got up the courage to try that one. My great grandmother used a little twig that she had chewed until it looked like a little brush to put the snuff inside her lip. As a bona fide tobacco chewer, I figured I didn't need any implements, just give me the snuff. I tried it and really didn't care for it but the tin was cool and, since I had paid for it, I was going to use it. I really couldn't get it to stay put in my mouth. It is so powdery that it just shifted around all the time, but I persevered. One day, while waiting outside a friend's house for him to come home, I decided it was time for a pinch of snuff. I dipped the appropriate amount out and packed it between my cheek and gum and layed back in the truck seat to wait. At some point in there I must have fallen asleep because at some other point I woke up. After I woke up, it occurred to me that I no longer had any snuff. As I pondered what might have happened to my tobacco, I sneezed. Powdery snuff blew out of my nostrils like Puff the Magic Dragon. It is hard to vomit with smoke coming out of your nose, but it can be done. I hated to waste $1.25, but I did. I did however, keep the cool tin.

As I said before, things were different then. The Ten Commandments and Bibles were welcome in school and guns weren't. Roe vs. Wade were your options when it came to fishing for flounder. I had no idea what cholesterol or carbohydrates were and wouldn't have cared even if I did know. Good meals were fried and covered in gravy and most had either been grown or raised yourself. Cell phones, laptops, GPS, ATM's, VCR's, DVD's and IPOD's weren't even heard of. We had a grand total of three TV channels and the kids stood at the set changing it until the parents decided what they wanted to watch. Not quite as efficient as a remote control but it taught you to stay outside or get snagged into channel checker duty. Movie theaters played cartoons before every movie, which was the only time you could see a cartoon other than early Saturday mornings. Businesses were closed on Sunday and sports didn't practice on Wednesday because that was church night. Everyone seemed to know their place and were content to be there. Your "Place" wasn't defined by your color, sex, age or anything else, it was determined by where you felt comfortable and if you chose another "Place", you were free to pursue it. We had bottled water, only it was an old Coke bottle that we filled with water and kept in the refrigerator but, most of the time, we drank out of the water hose outside. We all drank after each other and none of us ever died from it. By far the best part of that time and place was the people you met. There seemed to be more colorful characters then. People said things that most folks would find offensive today but, at that time, we were happy enough not to be offended and nice enough to forgive those giving offense. It really was a different time.

Time has a way of fading the clarity the things I should remember (taking out the trash) but only seems to enhance the memories of the characters I met in those hay fields and barns of my childhood. I'd like to share some of the more memorable ones with you.

Cowboy was an odd fellow. He was German with most of the alphabet in his name minus the vowels. I think there might have been one vowel but can't be sure. He was long and lanky with faded blue jeans and worn out boots with pointy toes. His belt buckle indicated that at some time he had, at least, participated in a rodeo. He stretched out 160 pounds over a six foot three inch frame. He didn't stand up as much as he unfolded. His beard always had a three day shadow which only made his bony face seem all the more hollow. He had huge, round eyes that were always wide open and gave the appearance that someone had just sneaked up and surprised him. Jutting out between his eyes was a long, thin nose which, came to a very sharp point at the end. If you could make a man into a mosquito, like they do in the sci-fi movies, it would have looked like Cowboy. He always wore a khaki work shirt with a ring in the pocket indicating the home of a can of snuff. I mention the snuff ring because I never saw him dip. In fact, clinched on one side of his mouth there always sat a cigar which, I only mention because I never saw him smoke. Instead, he chewed it constantly. The cigar moved with his mouth as he spoke which could prove to be quite distracting. With a flick of his mouth, he could move the cigar to the other side without missing a beat. I tried that but never could get it so I gave up.

The oddest part of Cowboy's attire was the felt cowboy hat that always sat atop of his greasy head. For those of you not familiar with cowboy hats, let me point out that most folks wear straw hats in the summer and felt in the winter since felt hats don't breathe much. Cowboy always wore his felt hat. It appeared to have been either white or gray at some previous time but now was a dirty brown with a dark black sweat ring around it. The brim also had a black streak running from the sweat ring to the edge of the brim where sweat would drip when Cowboy bent over to pick up something. Cowboy was quite the handsome fellow. He looked like a cartoon character in a Western comic book. Besides being funny looking, he also had some curious habits. He drank coffee all day, even in the summer time and he always brought his lunch. Bringing lunch to your work isn't strange but his meals were. They always included potted meat or sardines, both of which gave him gas. When we would take a break, he would go to his truck and break out a can of sardines and then proudly announce that he was working up a good crop of air biscuits. Whoever got stuck stacking hay with him in the barn after lunch was in for a treat. The man could fart like a pack mule. He had enough of an accent to make it difficult to understand him and the cigar sure didn't help any. Cowboy appeared to be about sixty and his old Ford truck looked even older than that. He had a colorful story for every dent in it and most of those stories included a healthy portion of cuss words and Pabst Blue Ribbon beer. I made the mistake of riding with him to a different pasture once. He had beer bottle tops on both radio dials and the inside of the truck had the unmistakable odor of cabbage. Cabbage and the Texas sun are not really a good combination in case you are wondering. A lariat hung from the gun rack on top of a single shot rifle that he called "Ellie". Cowboy seemed to believe that duct tape could fix anything and his seat covers were a testament to that theory. The gear shifter on the floor went unused as he had modified the original transmission with a three on the tree column gear shifter. An old pair of spurs hung around the base of the unused floor shifter and there were empty boxes of chicken wings and beer cans all over the floor. His missing gas cap had been replaced by a red bandana and his whip antennas both had a Houston Oilers figurine riding on the top of them. While the sight of the truck was impressive, it had nothing on the smell. At least he rode with the windows down.

Work in hay fields and barns in the summer was not especially pleasant and the folks who took to that kind of work had to be fairly tough. The mosquitoes alone were enough to drive you into another line of work. Most of the "hands" were usually young men in their late teens and early twenties and old cowboys so it came as quite a shock to me the day that I was behind a green Chevy truck with a man about thirty and two young boys. The boys were about twelve and ten. At the time I wasn't much older but at least I was full grown. The youngest boy drove while the father threw the hay in the truck and the oldest boy stacked. Stacking is the worst job of the bunch. A good stacker can fit those bales together as tight as a jigsaw puzzle that won't fall apart in a hurricane and a bad stacker can stack the same bales and they will blow over if a gnat sneezes on them. This, of course, requires re-stacking and doing the same work twice while getting paid once is not the best way to earn a living. I was lucky enough to have a partner who loved to stack. Not wanting to steal his joy, I let him. I was pretty sure that boy's hay would never make it to the barn but, as the morning wore on, their pace stayed fairly even with ours and they never lost a bale. They pulled into the barn just ahead of us and we patiently waited for them to unload. This provided a chance to get a drink of water and take a quick break. Once in the barn, both boys threw bales to the father and he stacked.

I would like to clarify my earlier statement. Stacking is the worst job in the hayfield and stacking in the barn, which technically is still stacking, is the worst of the worst jobs. What little shade the barn provides is greatly overshadowed by the choking heat and the stale air. You can literally see the air, it's full of black dust that sticks in your nostrils and throat. You cough it up for a couple of days. The barn also blocks all wind and provides a perfect place for the mosquitoes to live. You can't begin in imagine the size of the mosquitoes along the Gulf Coast. As Cowboy so eloquently put it, "Them bloodsuckers kin stand flatfooted and rape a turkey". Now I don't know whether Cowboy came to this conclusion as the result of his own scientific study or that was just his opinion, but it sure painted a graphic mental image.

When the father and his two boys had finished unloading the last bale, the father walked over to the fellow with the money to get paid. I don't know if the money-man was the owner or foreman but I did know that he had the money and that is really all we were concerned with. While he was getting paid, I offered the oldest boy a drink from our water jug. It was the latest in water cooling technology, an old milk jug filled with water and frozen the night before. We all drank from it and didn't even wipe the lid. That was before our lives were driven by the overwhelming fear of germs and diseases. It was so hot that it probably wouldn't have mattered if we knew about communicable diseases. I said, "Say hoss, would you like a drink of water?" as I offered the jug. "Yessir" he replied and then "Thanks". I had never been called "Sir" and wasn't too sure that I cared for it. I wasn't but just a few years older than he was but I knew better than to correct him and was pretty sure that, if his dad was anything like mine, not saying "Sir" would have been way worse than me correcting him so I let it go. I offered some to the younger boy who gladly accepted it. I went back to my truck as their father approached and I watched him count out a couple of bills for each boy. They lit up like a Christmas tree when he put the bills into their hands. The youngest boy said, "Daddy, can we stop and get a Coke on the way home", "Sure" his father answered, "But you're buying" and then he tossled the boy's blond mop and for the first time since I laid eyes on him, he looked like a little boy. I've always wondered about those boys and whatever became of them. They were not afraid of work and had good manners and that is a pretty good start in this old world.

By far, the most memorable character I met in those hayfields was El Roi (pronounced Elroy). I met him on my first, official job interview. I had worked several jobs by then but always for a neighbor or someone I knew from church. This was a real interview. We had driven by the day before and seen the baler in the pasture spitting out square bales behind it. My buddy and I got my mom to drop us off at the owner's barn the next morning hoping to find gainful employment. We got there shortly before 8:00 am. There were already a couple of guys with trucks and trailers waiting to go to work and I hoped we weren't too late. My buddy was born big. I tried my entire life to grow and he just came out that way. We looked like one and a half standing next to each other and I was afraid he wouldn't want to hire a couple of kids, even if one was as big as an oak. The owner was an older man in jeans with a very clean white, straw hat. He looked at my buddy and grinned (I was used to that) and then looked over at me a little less enthusiastically. He said, "You boys reckon you can throw those hay bales into the truck?". "Yessir" we replied in stereo. Then he grabbed my biceps like he was testing the strength of an old rope and said, "You've been in the field before haven't you boy?". I was pretty happy about him recognizing that I was a veteran of hard work, but wasn't very happy about being called "boy". I was trying hard to look grown and had a decent mustache coming in nicely. I just nodded trying to act nonchalant like I routinely met with potential employers on a regular basis. "See the old man in the barn, he'll put you both to work", and my interview was over.

We waived mom off (it's not really cool to have your mom drop you off at work but we were only 14) and went over to the barn. El Roi was sending different groups out to various pastures and we had to wait until he was done to get our marching orders. He was a sight. He was the blackest human being I had ever laid eyes on. He wore lace-up work boots, blue Dickie pants and a khaki work shirt with sleeves rolled up past his forearms. His forearms looked like two huge smoked hams with catchers mitts for hands. He just looked strong. He wasn't much taller than me but he had the air of a man who had worked hard all of his life and I truly believed that he could have wadded me up and put me in his pocket if he had taken a mind to. He wore a ball cap from the local feed store with the brim absolutely flat. It was quite stylish in those days to round the brim of your ball cap but I guess that style hadn't quite made its way into El Roi's wardrobe. His whole face smiled when he talked revealing a handful of teeth scattered about his mouth and I knew the minute that I saw him that I liked him. By the time he got through sending out the other hands, we were the only three left in the barn. As usual, his eyes lit up when he saw my buddy and then he looked at me. He never commented on our age or my size, he only asked if we had a partner or truck and trailer. Of course, we had neither. "C'mon with me, boys and ol' El Roi will put you to work" he said. We followed like puppies and he took us to his truck and trailer. It turned out to be a ranch truck and he was going to be our third hand. Despite being young, I was already quite the business man and knew that him driving the company truck could pay huge dividends. On other jobs, if you didn't own the truck and trailer, you usually had to give gas money to the guy who owned it. Working with El Roi, we got to keep all that we earned. Gas wasn't three dollars a gallon then but it wasn't free either and we both like the idea of keeping our entire check. I'd like to interject at this point that I got married a few years after that and haven't seen any of my paycheck since then.

El Roi drove us a little ways from the barn but still inside the same pasture as the barn where we would pick up hay. Turns out that working for El Roi meant you got the pick of the pastures as well. Being closer to the barn meant that you had less travel time, meaning more time picking up hay, meaning more money. When we stopped to pick up hay, El Roi offered to let me drive first and then said we could switch later. I didn't know how old he was but it seemed wrong to have an old guy throwing hay when I was driving besides, I wanted to prove that I could hold my own with the rest of the hired hands and I told El Roi that he could drive. He would have none of it. He said, "Boy, never forget that I'm the H.N.I.C. and I decide who does what". My buddy and I both looked at each other having no idea what "H.N.I.C" meant and I was the one foolish enough to ask. "That means Head Negro In Charge" he replied with a laugh. Of course, he used a much more colorful term than "Negro" but, like I said, things were just different then. It was settled, I drove. After our first load, I offered to switch and he took me up on it. While we were eating our lunch (it might not have been cool to have your mother drop you off at work but it was really cool having her pack you a big lunch) I asked El Roi how old he was. He said he didn't rightly know but thought that he was somewhere between 65 and 70. I had never met anyone who didn't know how old they were before. I thought that maybe he couldn't do the math so I asked what year he was born in and, again, he said he didn't know. He did know that he was born in March and could remember riding from Louisiana to Texas in a buckboard wagon with his parents and five brothers and sisters. He almost cried when he talked about the little sister he called "Sissy" that they buried before they left Louisiana. Every story made me want to ask a million more questions and the answers only made me want to hear more stories. When he spoke, he sounded like some of the older, black preachers I had heard and his voice had a melodic quality to it that made his stories sound more like songs that stories. He wasn't trying to entertain, he just couldn't help it.

After the second full day of working with El Roi, my buddy and I convinced him that a man of his status and position (after all, he was the H.N.I.C) should be driving while the young bucks like us should be throwing the hay. He reluctantly agreed. At first, he would ride with the window down giving directions and making sure that we didn't miss any bales and got them stacked good and tight. After he was fairly confident that we didn't need constant directions, he decided that it would be alright if he listened to the radio while he drove. AM was all there was to choose from and El Roi was fond of old country music. He would sing right along with Hank Sr., Charlie Pride, Ferlin Husky or whoever else came on. While his story telling voice sounded musical, his singing voice did not. We encouraged him to go back to giving us directions but he just kept on singing. Somewhere in there, he decided that we no longer needed directions and he rolled up the window and turned on the A/C. Normally, the driver just puts the truck in first and then lets it go at its own pace so the hay thrower and stacker can keep up. Unfortunately, as El Roi got to enjoying the music, the pace would pick up and we would have to bang on the side of the truck to get his attention to slow down. Fortunately for us he liked county music, if he had liked rock he would have ran us to death before we ever made it to 15.

We hauled all of the hay that had been cut and then El Roi asked us if we were interested in staying on for the next cut. Always anxious to earn cash we agreed and the next day he took us to a leased pasture where they were just finishing baling cane hay. Cane hay is at the bottom of the list as far as hay goes. It grows down in low bottoms that frequently hold water in that part of the country and the sticky sap in it draws ants and rats and every other nasty critter that you really don't want to stick your hands into. In the week that we worked that pasture, I found three dead possums and one live rattlesnake that had been caught and baled. The ants had infested every bale and about every other one had either a live or dead rat. The moist air and heat did nothing for the smell but El Roi's stories and the regular paycheck made the work a little more enjoyable. One day El Roi told us that he had to "git a holt of hisself", his little nickname for going to the restroom, and he went off behind an ancient oak tree. When he came back, I noticed that his zipper was down. "Your drawers are unzipped", I told him helpfully. "Don't worry boy, if it can't get up, it can't get out" he said with a straight face. My buddy and I laughed until we needed to "git a holt of ourselves" too. Life made El Roi laugh and he returned the favor to everyone he met. We worked most of the summer on that ranch and always with El Roi. We were his "boys" and from time to time he would take us to get a Cherry soda or a malt and he even sprang for a hamburger once but he said my buddy was too big to feed full time so we only got to do that once. El Roi had a story for everything and a saying about every natural phenomenon that occurred. If there was heavy moss growing on the tree it meant that it was going to be a cold winter and if the squirrels were out late in the morning picking up acorns it meant that it was sure to rain and so on. I imagine that El Roi has long since joined his Sissy in that great beyond as he used to call it but, from time to time, when I see the ranchers cutting hay, I stop and get a Cherry soda and drink one for El Roi.

PET PEEVES

By now you know far more about me than you would care to. The last thing that I would like to share with you is what really makes me mad. Then, you will know way more about me than you ever wanted to. You can learn a lot about a person when you know what makes them angry. I am not sure what this says about me, but I don't think it's good. So, here we go, the list of things that really torque me off.

1. Number one of all time is hearing women complain about the toilet seat being left up. If they sit on it and fall in that is their fault. I look before I go, they can too. You don't hear men saying, "I wish they'd leave that lid up so I would quit wetting on the seat". If we wet a closed lid, every woman in America would have us declared incompetent and moved into a cage where we could be hosed down. We look why can't they?
2. I hate it when people call my house and then ask who they are speaking to. If you don't know who you're calling, don't call. It also burns me up when you answer the phone and they say, "I'll bet you don't know who this is". I don't want to guess. I didn't even want to answer the phone but it wouldn't quit making noise until I did answer it.
3. I can't stand littering.
4. I hate buffet lines. I stood in line for eight years in the Navy. If I pay for food, I want it delivered to me.
5. While I am fundamentally cheap, there are certain items that should never be skimped on. I hate cheap cheese, chocolate, soft drinks and, most of all, toilet paper.
6. I hate answering machines. If I wanted to talk to a machine, I would discuss politics with my lawn mower.

7. I loathe ties. They serve no purpose. They don't keep you warm, make you cool or protect you from rain, they are just there for looks. I hate things that are just for looks.

8. It really makes me mad when a restaurant adds in a tip. If I want to tip, I will. If the clown is a lousy waiter, no tip. No freebies.

9. I can't stand self-righteous ex-smokers. I don't smoke. Don't even like to be around smokers, but I really don't want a speech about my lungs from some idiot that used to burn up his own carcass.

10. I don't like automated anything. After pencils and horses, life was all downhill.

11. I truly hate hearing computer weenies talk about computer weenie stuff. I don't want to hear about megabytes, ram or giga-anything. And just for the record, all the computer weenies that I know spend more time playing video games than expanding their ram, I can get the same thing from a Nintendo.

12. I hate shopping. What more can possibly be said about that?

13. The worst creature on the face of the Earth is a left-wing, liberal, tree hugger. I won't say that I hate them, but they aren't very far up on my Christmas card list.

14. I hate cards. See chapter regarding same.

15. I hate flowers. Not the pretty kind you see in a garden or on the side of the road, I'm talking about the kind you pay big bucks for to give to your wife. They are dead for crying out loud. If I pay for something that is dead, it should be on a plate.

16. I get tired of child rearing advice from people whose expertise comes from their dog fluffy. While the mess they make looks and smells the same, that is where the similarities end. People without kids always seem to know just how to raise your kids.

17. I hate advice that I don't ask for. I know that I don't know everything, so I go to someone who does know what I want to know. If I don't ask you, then I obviously don't think you know.

18. I hate loud car radios.

19. I hate trucks that don't have dirt on them. It's like having a hammer that is too pretty to hit a nail with.

20. I despise the word "ill". I don't get ill. I get full fledged sick. "Ill" doesn't do justice to heaving up your guts.

21. I really don't like women in hats, it makes them look like Annie Oakley.

22. I don't like women in men's suits, it makes them look like men.

23. I really don't like men in women's clothes. No further comment.

24. With all that is within me, I hate political correctness.

25. I hate golf. It is fine so long as it doesn't interrupt a football game.

26. I hate broccoli. If God wanted me to eat grass, I would have cloven hooves.

27. Lawyers, insurance companies, and phone salesmen. Need I say more?

28. I can't stand people who think they know everything. They interfere with those of us who really do.

29. I hate fashion. Fashion changes but ugly remains the same whether it is in style or not.

30. I hate potpourri.

31. I really hate it when the waist size on a man's pants is smaller then the length. If you are fat and wear blue jeans, you know exactly what I am talking about.

32. I also hate soap operas. They are a complete insult to the intelligent mind. If you have to watch rich people have problems to feel better about yourself, you really need to get a life.

33. My final pet peeve is dedicated to a dear friend who reads the end of a book first. Why, oh why, would anyone do that? This removes the emotional involvement required to enjoy a good book (unlike this one). It spoils the entire book. I won't even lend my friend a book because I know they will read the end first. I don't know why that should bother me so, but it does. I realize that I have let it become an obsession and, for this reason, I made this the last chapter.

For all of you who read the last chapter first, I wanted to make sure that you read something worth reading. To start, let me quote another writer, the disciple John who said, "For God so loved the world, that He gave his only begotten Son, that whosoever should believe in Him should not perish, but have everlasting life" John 3:16. The Apostle Paul tells us, "That if thou shalt confess with thy mouth the Lord Jesus, and shalt believe in thine heart that God hath raised Him from the dead, thou shalt be saved" Romans 10:9. I have greatly enjoyed sharing stories from my past with you, but I would enjoy much more sharing my Savior with you. If you have never asked Jesus Christ into your heart, I pray that you will take this moment to stop and recognize that He is the missing ingredient in your life. God doesn't want you to be worthy, He wants you to be willing. Take this moment to ask Christ to come into your heart and forgive you for all of your sins and let Him take care of the rest. If you only read this, I know that you will have read something worth reading. I've enjoyed spending time with you, I hope you have in enjoyed it as well. If you get there before I do, tell Paul I said, "Hello". God Bless.

B.B. Howard